TALES & TIME

Lost Time Academy: Book One

G. BAILEY

USA TODAY BESTSELLING AUTHOR

TALES & TIME

EVEN THE DARKEST FAIRYTALES COME TRUE...

G. Bailey

USA TODAY BESTSELLING AUTHOR

Join Bailey's Pack

Join <u>Bailey's Pack</u> on Facebook to stay in touch with the author, find out what is coming out next and any news!

www.gbaileyauthor.com

❊ Created with Vellum

Description

What if all the fairy tales are real? What if you were one of them?
When Madilynn turned seventeen, her parents dropped a big, ancient-looking book in her lap and said to open it by herself. Madilynn almost wishes she hadn't when it reveals she is a descendant of a fairy tale, and her parents tell her it's time for her to attend Lost Time Academy.
Being thrown into a world that is literally full of fairy tales, the last thing she expects is to see the four guys she grew up with.
Four guys who have grown from boys to now geeky, dark, passionate men who rule the Academy…and they never forgot Madilynn.
Time makes all tales come true, including the dark ones.

Reverse harem & 17+

Dedication

To sleep. I really think you are my soulmate, and that we should spend more time together.

WHEN THE RAVENS COME.
THE ANCIENT TALES WILL
SUCCUMB.
THE RAVEN CROWS.

THE RAVEN KNOWS.

WHEN THE RAVEN DIES.
SLEEP WILL ARISE.

FOR SLEEP AND WAR ARE
DESTINED FOR ONLY RUIN.
THE RAVEN WILL FALL.
THE WORLD WILL SLEEP

FOR ONLY A BEAUTY CAN
SURVIVE THE DEEP SLEEP.

Prologue

I laugh as I dance around, losing myself to the music and eventually losing Tavvy and Ella in the crowd as I move away, avoiding other students. I drink my beer, hating the taste as I move my hips and slowly put my hands above my head, swaying to the music that seems to speak to me. I put the beer on a table somewhere before swaying my hips to a slower song in the middle of a big bunch of dancing people.

"Hey, party girl," a guy whispers into my ear before roughly pulling me back to him, his hands tightening around my waist before I can move away.

"Let go," I demand, trying to push him away from me, but it doesn't work, and he just holds me tighter. I try to wriggle out of his grip as he presses his head next to mine and kisses my ear. I start to feel my power in my fingertips just before the arms are ripped away from me, and I stumble a little as I try to stand up straight. I turn to see Knox holding a wiry young man in the air by the back of his jacket, but Knox's angry eyes are on me. There is silence as Knox lifts a beefy fist and punches the guy hard in the face. The jerk falls to the floor with a smack, and he doesn't get up. It should scare me, but the whole alpha thing just seems to do the opposite. *I like this side to Knox.* He is definitely the darkest one of the brothers now. The music is suddenly cut off as Knox walks to me in big strides and swiftly picks me up, throwing me over his shoulder before I can protest about it.

"Let me make this clear while you are all listening. Madilynn Dormiens belongs to the Tale brothers. Anyone touches her, and they deal with us."

Chapter 1

*T*he squawking of dozens of crows makes my eyes shoot open, seeing the green grass I'm lying on as it brushes against my cheek. It's so dark that it's all I can think about as I lift my head. I can hear the terrible squawking above me, it's so loud that I can't do anything but look where it's coming from. I search the dark sky and see the dozens of crows flying in circles around my head. They fly in a circle, so I can only just see the stars through the wings and black feathers that fall around me. The cold wind blows against the black dress I'm wearing, and I can smell fire in the distance. I reach a hand out as the feathers suddenly start catching fire around me, the wind making them swirl around me in a vortex of fire and feathers.

"Sleep and save, sleep and save," the words seem to come from the crows, but I know that's impossible because crows can't talk. The words just keep getting louder, mixing with the *squawking, the fire, and the feathers until everything is a blur. I hold my hands over my ears as it gets impossible to even think over the noise, and I scream.*

"*H*appy birthday," my parents shout in unison as they walk into my bedroom, waking me up from another weird dream that I try to forget. Again. I've been having dreams of crows and the same thing for over a year, and the dreams just get more and more real. Not that any of it makes sense, and I'm not about to explain the dreams to my parents; it would just freak them out.

"I can't believe the day is finally here," my mum says, looking excited as I sit up in bed. My mum doesn't look her age, but it likely has something to do with how beautiful she is. Everyone says we look similar as I have her chocolate brown hair and matching brown eyes, but I don't see it otherwise. I'm average looking compared to my mum, I think, though my boyfriend disagrees. My mum is the beauty queen who loves make-up and dresses, and I'm the tomboy who prefers messy buns and my favourite Dorito-stained hoodie. My dad has wavy blond hair and a constant playful expression, even this early in the morning. It's clear they both just got out of bed, as they are still in their dressing gowns, and I wonder for a second how anyone can be so bouncy so damn early.

"What day is it?" I say, yawning as I try to come around to reality and the fact I'm not sleeping when I should be.

"Your birthday, of course! We need you to open this, alone, and then come to find us. We will answer everything then," my mum cryptically states, and I just gape at her. My parents have never woken me up with presents in my room…this is weird. They usually give me chocolate cake with candles on it in bed and presents later. Yet, there is no cake.

"We should have brought her a cup of coffee. She looks like a zombie from *The Walking Dead*," my dad chuckles, wrapping an arm around my mum's waist.

"What are you guys going on about? It's too damn early for riddles, dad," I reply with a groan, and dad just grins before turning around and heading out the door for a second. I flash my mum a confused look as she bounces on the spot in excitement, and I look back as dad returns with a big box. It's a present box wrapped in light blue paper.

"Just open the present and then come down-stairs," he tells me and walks out the door with my mum, shutting it behind them. I'm seventeen, and there's no cake for breakfast like last year? *That sucks.* I look at the box and decide to have a shower before opening whatever is in there. I am hoping for a car, but that doesn't seem likely somehow with a box this size. I grab some clothes before showering and spending ages drying my long hair. *I need another haircut.* I look in the mirror and shrug at my pale complexion and freckle-covered face. Seventeen, and I still look like a kid. I glance at my phone when I come back into my bedroom, seeing dozens of Facebook messages from friends at school wishing me a happy birthday, when it suddenly rings. I smile at the handsome face of the screen before answering the call.

"Hey, Madi. Happy birthday!" Quinton, my boyfriend, says down the line in a cheery voice. He is one of those morning people too.

"Morning, Quin, and thank you," I reply, hearing his laugh.

"Are you eating chocolate cake yet?" he asks. Quinton has been my friend since we were little, and then we started dating a year ago when our friendship just turned into something more. I knew I loved him as more than a friend when he climbed through my window, like he did every weekend, but seeing him soaking wet from the rain he must have walked an hour in to get to my house, and the look I remember him giving me, changed things. That night changed everything between us, and neither of us would change a thing about it now. *I love him.*

"Nope, no cake today. I'm not happy," I say, making him chuckle.

"Aw, I will bring you cake later and your present," he replies.

"You didn't have to get me anything," I gently say.

"You're my girlfriend, so yeah I did," he tells me. To be honest, I would be happy with the cake as he really didn't need to get me anything. Quinton works part-time to afford food for himself and his mum, as she can't work. Not by choice, but her love of alcohol gets her fired from every job she has ever had, and the moment Quinton could work to help them, she didn't stop him.

"Meet you at school in an hour, yeah?" he asks. I look at the box on my bed, knowing I might as well open it and then escape to school to see Quin.

"Sure," I reply to him, yawning loudly. Maybe I could take a nap today as well.

"Oh, and Sleepy?" he says, using that damn nickname that he and only four other people made up once, and it stuck.

"Yes, Quin?" I reply, trying not to yawn to prove the nickname's point as I'm still tired.

"Actually, it doesn't matter. I'll tell you later. Bye, Sleepy," he says, his tone a little off. I frown as the line cuts off before I can reply to him. *I wonder why he is being weird?* I shake my head, sliding my phone into my back pocket as I walk back over to the box. I pick it up and sit on the bed before undoing the ribbon. I lift the lid off the box, and inside is an old gold book. *That is certainly not a car.* The book has a symbol on the front that is a half-moon in a circle with flowers and swirls inside the moon. There's a cat drawing sitting on the moon, its head looking up at the top of the moon. *Why the hell would they give me an old book with a cat on it, when I'm allergic to cats?* Actually, I'm more than just allergic. Cats have a habit of going crazy when I'm near them and trying to bite or chase me. Cats are my enemies… and my parents know this.

I reach my hands in and pick the book up, surprised by how heavy it is as I place it on my lap after pushing the box onto the bed. I open the cover slowly; the pages are made of thick, soft material that I don't really recognize. The moment I look down at the first page, it starts to glow a soft gold colour, and my hands suddenly feel locked onto the book as the gold glow starts travelling over my hands. I scream in a panic, trying to let the damn book go, but it doesn't work; my hands feel tied to the book no matter what I do. I stand up, trying to shake the book away, but that doesn't work. I hear a strange, sweet noise as I run to the door then look down at the open book as I realise the book is making the sound. The book starts to get blurry only seconds before I feel myself falling back while hearing a deep voice shouting words so fast I can just barely catch them:

Two hundred years since the last descendant rose, and a beauty that only sleeps is found. For sleep makes beauty possible, and sleep is needed to break the curse. Only her heart can save us from the curse. Only a Sleeping Beauty descendant can stop what is to come.

I snap my eyes open and drop the book, moving back until I fall onto my bed and stare down at the book on the floor. *What the hell is wrong with it?*

When I move my arm to wrap it around myself, I realise it hurts slightly. Looking down, I see the half-moon in a circle tattooed in the middle of my wrist, the one off the cover of that book—and the damn cat on it. *I have a cat tattoo when cats hate me... flipping brilliant.* Quin is going to laugh his head off or think I'm crazy when I explain how I got it. I've always wanted a tattoo, but not this way...or of a bloody cat of all things. I get off the bed, keeping my eyes on the creepy book until I get to the door, and only look away to open it. When I glance back at the book, it disappears into gold dust. I try not to scream as I run out the door like the book itself is chasing me. I jog down the stairs as fast as I can and into the kitchen where my mum is cutting a big chocolate cake on the counter.

"Oh my god, she is a descendant!" my mum exclaims as her eyes lock on me, and she runs over, pulling me into her arms. I look over at dad sat on the stool, reading his newspaper like he does every morning. Like nothing just happened. *What the flipping hell is a descendant?*

"What is going on, mum? What is that possessed book that gave me a tattoo and disappeared into dust?" I ask, pulling away from her. "Wait, that makes me sound crazy...but that book is not right!" My mum lets me go a little, squeezing my shoulders, and she looks over to my dad, clearly giving him a look that suggests he answer.

"It's our family book, and it is not possessed. The book is just full of ancient magic from the first of our kind. It appears on the birthday of every descendant in our line and disappears when they have opened it," he says and then turns the page in his newspaper like he is explaining an everyday event.

"That makes a lot of sense," I say drily, and he laughs loudly, finally putting the paper down.

"So, what is the damn cat and moon tattoo on my wrist? Is someone going to explain the tattoo with another crazy story?" I ask, holding out my wrist, and my parents look at each other with a small smile.

"Yes, we will," my mum states, sounding proud and glancing at my wrist. "Your grandmother is going to be so happy, she thought that you might get the powers one day," mum says with a massive smile.

"No, we will never hear the end of how your mother was right—again—you mean," Dad groans.

"What powers? Can someone just explain what the hell is going on?" I snap, placing my hands on my hips, and mum puts an arm around my shoulders in comfort. Even with how freaked out I am, my parents just instantly calm me somehow.

"Let's go and sit down. It's a long story and one I have waited so long to tell you, Madi," she says gently. *I have a feeling whatever this story is might change everything.*

Chapter 2

"Fairy tales are real," my dad states first before my mum can speak as he sits on the sofa opposite me. My mum hands me a glass of water as I gape at dad's words, before she goes to sit next to him. I almost nervously laugh until I spot my dad's serious expression.

"You must be joking," I suggest, and he shakes his head with a huff. But my dad jokes about a lot of things, so clearly this must be one of them. Fairy tales aren't real. There is no wolf in the woods that eats girls with red cloaks on their way to grandma's house. There is no prince looking for a cleaner who lost her slipper at midnight at his ball.

"Not at all, sweetheart. I'm going to tell you our family history, and then you can ask me questions," he tells me, and I nod, not knowing what to say anyway. I don't want to believe him, but then I keep thinking about the glowing book and the words I heard, not that they made much sense. I've also never known my dad to lie to me. Mum was the one who told me the stories about the tooth fairy and Santa, and Dad was the one who told me they weren't real when I asked. My dad doesn't lie to me, and that makes this whole situation so much more serious. I glance down at my wrist which still slightly stings from the damn cat tattoo, and I know I can't just pretend this isn't happening. That this isn't real.

"There once were three goddesses, all sisters and *very* powerful. The oldest sister made the humans and gave life to earth and every living thing in it. The second sister became jealous of the first and her love for the humans, so she created humans with powers, dark powers, and they started killing the humans in jealousy of their simple lives with no curses. The first goddess died trying to protect her humans, but it was no use. Over time, the dark humans had children who hunted the remaining humans for sport, forcing them into hiding. The third sister, who was the quiet one, never chose a side between her sisters. However, when she heard the oldest sister died, she knew something had to be done to stop the whole of earth being destroyed. So she created the originals, the fairy tales, as humans came to know them. They said she blessed three hundred of the hiding human families with powers, and they fought back against the dark ones and kept the peace on earth after. The dark ones are marked with a circle with an eye in the middle, and a wolf sitting on the eye. The originals have the moon and cat tattoo which you now have," he tells me this tale of goddesses, fairy tales and things I never believed in as I rub a finger over my own tattoo. I'm a descendant of this goddess. That is what my dad is telling me.

"What happened to the two sisters after?" I ask. I'm pretty sure two powerful goddesses don't just disappear.

"No one knows that, but we believe they must have died at some point," he tells me before continuing. "Maybe they decided to give the creatures they created some peace."

"The originals had children, some received powers and others did not. The ones who did not also had children, and some of their children received powers. This went on for many years, with original generations being lost in the fight against the dark ones who kept breeding as well," my dad says, and my mum gives me a sad look as a shiver travels across my skin.

"Dark ones are still alive?" I quietly ask.

"Yes. We never told you any dark fairy tales growing up, but surely you must know some from school or movies," my mum suggests gently, and I nod, thinking of any fairy tales I can and somewhat trying to push them from my mind.

"Which one of you are descendants? I'm assuming you, mum, if grandmother knows about all this," I say.

"Both our families are descendants, darling. My mother has powers, and her mother before, but not me," mum tells me, and I pick up the slight sadness in her tone and the way dad wraps an arm around her shoulders.

"You think I have your family powers?" I ask in a whisper, and mum goes to answer when dad pats her leg and leans forward on his seat, stopping her from whatever she was going to say.

"What did the book say to you?" my dad asks me, and I think back to the creepy words the book said. I don't remember it all, it was all too much at the time, and I have a feeling I might regret that at some point.

"Something about sleep, and two hundred years, and a curse," I say, and my dad grins. "I don't really know what else. It was said too quickly."

"That's my family then," he says, and mum

nods with her own smile as she looks between us, but her eyes seem somewhat worried.

"There hasn't been a descendant with powers in two hundred years in my family line," dad says, and he looks so proud that I almost smile at him. There is no worry in my dad's eyes.

"What are the family powers? What am I a descendant of?" I ask, almost not wanting to hear the answer.

"Your last name answers that, hunny," mum says, and one of the reasons I have my nickname is my last name translates into sleep. *And I like to sleep a lot.*

"Well, the family name and descendant name is Dormiens, but you might be more familiar with the fairy tale called Sleeping Beauty. We should have guessed with how many times you've been put into detention for falling asleep in class at school," dad laughs, and he has a point. *It may have happened once or fifty times, but who's counting?*

"You're saying I'm Sleeping Beauty's descendant?" I ask, thinking of the fairy tale. A beautiful girl sleeps for hundreds of years after pricking her thumb on a wheel, and then a prince kisses her awake. I always thought Sleeping Beauty should have punched the random stranger who snuck into her room and kissed her when she was sleeping.

Though not a lot of people thought that when we watched it in school. *Wasn't Sleeping Beauty blonde as well?* I lift a strand of my dark hair, twirling it around my finger. I'm sure there was a dragon or evil witch or something in the movie…I hope that was just the movie. I don't think I've ever read or googled the original Sleeping Beauty fairy tale before. I clearly need to get my fairy tale books out or watch some Disney films.

"Yes. I'm not sure exactly what your gifts are, as the last family member who had your gifts died in an accident a day after she got them. There isn't any record of our family powers, but we know it has a lot to do with sleep," dad states, shrugging his shoulders like that isn't a big deal. What the hell could I do? Put myself to sleep whenever I want? I've had that "power" for years.

"This explains why she never gets up in the morning," mum says with a grin, and I just look at her. *Seriously, mum?*

"What?" she replies, rolling her eyes. "When you were a baby, you slept nearly all the time. I used to get so worried!"

"Why didn't you tell me about all of this? Prepare me for this world you've just thrown me into blind? Why tell me right now?" I ask in annoyance. This isn't something you hide for no reason.

"We are bound by our laws not to tell you until you turn seventeen and touch the book. It's the way of the descendants, our people. *Your people.* One day when you marry, you will make the same vow to never tell your own child," Dad tells me firmly, not one ounce of apology on his face. "Besides, you got to live a human life…a normal one with friends and routine. I would never have told you anything until this moment because I would have always wanted a normal upbringing for you."

"I suppose it's hard to be mad at you when you put it like that," I mumble, and dad laughs.

"I'd hold off on stating you're not mad. You have to leave here tonight," dad tells me, not giving me any time to process any of this before dropping another bomb on me.

"Leave to go where?" I ask hesitantly. I have a feeling he means leaving home.

"Lost Time Academy," he says with a big smile.

"What the hell is that?" I ask and then pretty much answer my own question when they don't say a word. "Are you seriously sending me to a boarding school? You want me to leave home now?"

"It's a school for the descendants to safely learn their gifts. Everyone from the ages of seventeen to twenty-one goes if they receive powers, and there isn't a choice here, Madilynn," mum tells me, using her strict tone that anyone who knows her doesn't want to hear. Usually I would be scared and agree with her, but not at the moment.

"I'm not going," I say, crossing my arms and raising an eyebrow at her angry expression. Dad takes mum's hand into hers, whispering something under his breath that I can't hear, and my mum just calms down nearly instantly.

"You have to go, Madi. We don't want our only child to go away, but we wouldn't send you unless we had no choice," dad tells me.

"I have a life here, a boyfriend I can't just disappear on," I tell him, thinking of Quinton.

"He is human, and the council of descendants will never let you stay friends with or marry a human. Our marriages are planned and told to us not long after we open the book. Whoever is chosen for you won't let you have a human friend who you used to date. I'm sorry, Madi," he says, and I just glare at him. This just keeps getting better and better. First off, I'm not exactly just human. Then boarding school. Now arranged marriage, and I have to break up with Quin…this birthday sucks.

"You knew I would never be able to be with Quin, yet you let me date him?" I ask, not believing my parents would let me get hurt like this. I literally feel sick at the idea of leaving Quin. We've already lost four of my childhood friends, and Quin would never get over me walking away from him.

"We didn't let you; if I remember right, I walked in to get you for breakfast one morning and found you kissing the boy," my dad says. "We couldn't give you a reason not to date him back then, and we assumed it wouldn't last long."

"It's better to end the relationship now, darling. Your new life has no place for a human. You will hurt him far more in the long run if you drag the relationship out. You will be happy with whoever the council decides you should marry," mum says, her gaze is nothing but sorry, but pain shoots through my heart at the thought of dumping Quinton. Of not being with him.

"A planned marriage? Are you kidding me?" I spit out, because I can't deal with how my mum could be right. There is no way in hell that is happening.

"Not at all. Even those of us with no powers have our marriages chosen. That's how I met your mother," he tells me, and she smiles lovingly at him. "The council always picks successful marriages. The man that chooses is a descendant of Cupid, and he is never wrong." I almost go to question mum about how Cupid is a Greek god and not necessarily a fairy tale, but the panic about leaving Quinton over-rides anything else.

"It won't be that bad, and Quinton will under-stand," dad says, like Quin's and my relationship is nothing. I've known Quin my entire life, and even before we dated, I couldn't imagine my life without my best friend in it. I give my dad a nasty look. He never liked Quinton, and I guess I now know why.

"No, he won't." I say, knowing he is going to worry when I don't turn up for school. "I'm going to be late for school, I should—"

"No, Madilynn. You have powers now, powers that could hurt humans, and you have to pack for Lost Time Academy," Dad interrupts me as I stand up, and I pause, realising that I can't ignore this as much as I want to. This isn't going to go away, and I can't run from this. I can't run to Quin like I always have when something is wrong.

"I can't just disappear on him! I need to explain this to Quinton in person. Just let me go and—" I plead with them, wiping away the stray tears that fall down my cheeks, and my mum gives me a small shake of her head, looking just as upset. She practi-cally brought Quinton up with me. Quinton's mum never fed him, so at least three times a week, Quinton would be at ours for a meal. My mum even packs me two school lunches every day because she knows Quinton would share mine otherwise. Or I would give my lunch to Quin and be starving when I got home.

"You can't tell humans about us, your powers, or anything, Madilynn. That is a death sentence for you—and him. The world you have just joined is very strict about humans and wouldn't think twice about killing him, his whole family and anyone he could have told," Dad says, and I hold my hand over my mouth. I couldn't even think about losing Quinton, and even if we ran away, Quinton has family he cares for too much. Quinton has a younger sister who is only twelve. Even if she lives with her dad, they would kill her for knowing him, if my dad is right. Loving Quinton would get us all killed.

"No," I whisper, my whole body shaking as my mum swiftly gets up off the sofa and comes to me. I don't move, letting my mum pull me tightly into her arms as she tries to comfort me.

"You can stay his friend, in time. Only you will just tell him we got you into an exclusive boarding school that means you can't contact him for now," Dad suggests once mum lets me go and I have calmed down enough to even talk.

"Where is Lost Time Academy?" I ask quietly after a long pause between us all, where my heart feels like it's breaking into pieces, and yet, I know this is the right thing to do.

"In Ireland, and we will take a portal there tonight," dad simply replies.

"Portal?" I curiously ask.

"Every descendant family gets a key," he says, pulling out the small key on his necklace that he always wears. I remember asking him about it as a child, and he always said that it was a family thing and never said anymore.

"I have one too," mum says, showing me the bracelet with a small key hanging off it. Mum always wore the bracelet, and I never thought to ask about it as it looks fashionable and, well, normal.

"The key is a connection to the island where Lost Time Academy sits and many other buildings for our kind. It is the safest place, and every descendant knows to go there if anything goes wrong. You can take mine, and your mum can go with you. She can't enter the school, only descendants with powers can, but she can walk you to the door," my dad says, pulling off the necklace and handing it to me.

"You can't come too?" I lightly ask.

"No. Only one can travel with a key," he tells me gently, and I look down at the small gold key, the little "L" and a "T" that is engraved on the side. I never saw that before.

"Time makes all tales come true," my dad whispers, watching me run a finger over the key.

"What does that mean?" I ask him, looking up to meet my dad's eyes.

"The words engraved in the school symbol, but they are in Latin," he explains to me.

"Latin?" I ask.

"Oh yes. Everyone has to learn Latin at Lost Time Academy. It's not that bad once you get used to it," he adds when he sees my face of disgust. *Yes, it is that bad, but I'm not thinking of Latin, I'm thinking of leaving everything behind, including Quinton.*

Chapter 3

"It's time to leave," my mum says as I stare down at the text I'm about to send to Quinton, explaining everything, and every damn word of it is a lie. Every word I've written and rewritten a thousand times, and I haven't even got the strength to read the several messages he has sent me. Dad said I can't call him, that Quinton would be able to tell I'm lying over the phone as he knows me too well. *Dad is right.* Quinton knows me better than anyone. It doesn't stop me from wanting to press that call button though and hovering my finger over the silly contact picture I have of him. I press send on the text before I can think about him anymore, and a sharp pain feels like it rips through my chest when I imagine him opening it. I'm a coward; I should have called him. Then again, I can't ever risk his life, and my dad said I would be doing just that. *I don't have a choice anymore when it comes to Quinton.* I stand up, picking up my rucksack full of my clothes and things I need before walking to my mum where she is stood at the door. She smiles at me, and I look over at my dad, who comes over and hugs me tightly.

"Good luck, and I want a phone call every week if they allow it, or a letter perhaps. It has been a long time since I went to school, and we didn't have phones back then," he tells me, and I nod against his chest.

"If Quinton comes here, I don't know, just be nice to him please," I whisper, and dad grumbles.

"I will do, but I doubt the boy is going to be happy with us for sending you away," dad replies as he lets me go and steps back.

"I know," I say, feeling my phone vibrate in my hand. I turn it off before looking who it was. I don't know who I'm kidding as I know it's Quinton. I just broke up with him over text, of course he's going to try and call me. I swallow every part of me that wants to run out the door and find Quinton as I look at my parents' worried faces. After pushing my phone into my bag, I force a smile on my face as I wait for my mum to say something.

"Okay, take out your key and hold it in the air like this," she says and holds out the key like she is unlocking an imaginary door. I do the same and feel stupid as nothing happens, and I raise an eyebrow at her.

"Lost Time Island welcomes its blood," she whispers, her words sending shivers through me, and mum smiles at me. A gold light appears from her key and surrounds her whole body until she has disappeared completely. I'm sure I stand with my mouth hanging open for far too long before I snap it shut and look over at dad. He is trying not to laugh, and I just glare at him as he chuckles under his breath.

"Repeat her words and have fun at your new school. We will speak soon," my dad suggests after he stops laughing and acquires a more serious expression as he seems to realise I have to go now.

"Lost Time Island welcomes its blood," I repeat my mother's words, and all I can see is the gold light as it shines out the key that gets warmer in my hand until it feels like it is almost burning. I eventually have to close my eyes, blocking the light. After what feels like a few seconds, I feel a hand on my shoulder, and the light is suddenly gone. I open my eyes to see my mum right in front of me, and I lower my hand with the key. When I look past her and to the woods we are now stood in the middle of, it's almost unbelievable that we moved anywhere, but this makes it seem so real. I can smell the pine, feel the cold wind brushing my hair around, and hear the snapped branches under my feet as I shift. I pull my leather jacket closer around me; the leggings and top I'm wearing underneath are no good against the cold out here.

"You did well for your first time using the key. Don't repeat this, but your dad passed out," mum says with a wink as she squeezes my shoulder, making me chuckle. She nods her head in the direction behind her and turns before she starts walking off down a purple stone path through the woods. I catch up and follow her, putting my key, still on the chain, around my neck. The path is lit up by stones that lightly glow, they are cool and pretty to look at, but I'm sure I saw similar solar lights on sale at my local shop. I doubt the stones are real. Or maybe I am still trying to pretend everything is normal.

"I was thinking. What's your family descended from?" I ask my mum after we have walked in silence for a while.

"Oh, it's not a well-known one, but Crows. Have you heard of the rhyme about crows?" she asks, referring to the nursery rhyme. I nod. "Well, that's the closest humans got to our descendants' story. We have wings if we get that power, and it's meant to be unlucky. But your grandmother wins every week at bingo, so maybe that isn't so true," mum laughs, and I do as well. Grandma is super proud of her unbeatable score at bingo.

"But grandma doesn't have wings. I'm sure I would have noticed that," I comment, thinking of my slightly insane grandmother who I love to pieces. I usually stay at her house throughout the holidays as does Quinton because grandma loves him. I don't say "insane" lightly; she has done a lot of things over the years that people would consider completely crazy. But she is the kind of crazy that walks into a stranger's house, makes a cup of tea, and then cleans the house before she leaves. The nice kind of crazy you don't mind so much.

"She does have wings, but she clearly hides them from you," mum says with a shrug like it's nothing. Grandma has wings. *Next, she is going to tell me she has big teeth to eat me with.*

"Grandmother has wings, okay then," I mutter, and mum doesn't respond to my sarcastic reply but only grins over at me. I wrap my arms around myself more, wondering where exactly Lost Time Island is and why it is so cold. I honestly wouldn't be surprised to see snow falling with how cold it is.

"Can you get more than one descendant

power?" I ask, thinking of my dreams of crows I've been having. It's a strange thing to dream—or have nightmares—of when crows apparently have a lot to do with my heritage.

"No. It's impossible," she tells me just as a wave of fear hits me, making me want to run away. Sweat gathers on my forehead as my heart beats loudly in my chest, and my mouth goes dry. I start to take a step back, feeling the urge to run as my mum stands still. The fear of—well, nothing—is filling my mind, and I can't seem to think of anything other than the massive need to run away.

"Lost Time Island welcomes its blood. Madi-lynn Dormiens is here to start her first year," my mum shouts in a breathless voice, the only sign the overwhelming fear is affecting her. The feeling of fear disappears straightaway, making me take a deep breath and rest my hands on my knees as I bow my head.

"The ward makes you feel fear, darling. It makes humans walk the other way from here and wards off people who are not welcome," mum tells me, and it makes some sense. *It's a damn good alarm.* I guess you can't have humans just walking up to the gates of Lost Time Academy full of fairy tale descendants. The crunching of leaves makes me look up and straighten up as a man walks over. He has long black hair and dark eyes, but other than that, he is wearing a hoodie and jeans, looking like a normal guy in his mid-twenties I would think.

"The headmasters are ready to see you, Madilynn Dormiens. Please come with me," the man firmly suggests. His voice is much posher than his appearance, which is odd. I look over at my mum for her thoughts, and she nods once before we start following him down the path. The path opens up to a large bridge over a river, and we walk across it into an enormous stone courtyard full of benches. The academy is basically a massive house, a mansion made from grey stone and tall pillars with dozens of cracks in them. There are no people—at least none that I can see—as we walk past the benches and up the stairs to the entrance. I look up when I get to the top of the stairs, seeing the circle and moon symbol carved in stone on the door, with the damn cat painted in tinted glass. There is writing surrounding it, but I can't read it as it must be in Latin.

"I'm afraid only Miss Dormiens can enter," the man stops my mum to remind her as he stands in front of the door with his hand resting on it.

"Good luck, darling. I know you feel lost, but

maybe this is just where you are meant to be," mum says gently to me. "I will miss you very much." It's difficult to say goodbye to her; I feel like I'm leaving everyone I've ever cared about right now, and I couldn't think of a worse thing to do on my birthday.

"I will miss you, too," I reply, sniffling a little as she pulls away. "Wait, how will you get back home?" I ask her.

"We will make sure your mother is returned safely. Now come, the headmasters are waiting," the man says behind me in a strict voice, his tone suggesting he is tired of waiting. I let mum pull me into a tight hug once more.

"Be safe and beware of the ones you think you can trust," she says in a quiet whisper, and I nod against her shoulder, not understanding her warning but remembering it anyway. I watch as she walks back towards the forest before I grab my bag and turn to see the man open the doors and wave me in. I walk past him into the big entrance hall of the house which is old. *Very old and very dusty.* Everything from the dark wooden floors to the massive chandeliers with giant cobwebs on them screams deserted mansion. There are small sconces that line the walls, casting huge creepy-looking shadows everywhere. The lights even go up the huge staircase. The man walks to the left of the stairs, and I keep following him as I don't want to get lost in here. He leads me to a small corridor that is lined with doors, and between each door are old paintings in frames. I glance at the paintings, which are all old people in ancient clothes, before concentrating on where we are going once again.

The man knocks on the last door in the corridor before opening it and waving a hand for me to walk in. I enter, and he shuts the door behind me with a slight bow of his head. I look back into the room to face two women sat on chairs behind a desk. They both have grey hair in a tight bun, the moon and cat mark are in the middle of their foreheads, and their matching purple eyes watch me closely. They are twins and impossible to tell apart. They are literally identical in every sense. They both are wearing green cloaks that are tied at the neck by a silver clip that also dons the symbol. Another cat and moon. *Damn cats are everywhere.*

"Madilynn Dormiens, I presume?" the one on the left says, and I nod rather than answering one of the creepy twins.

"Please sit," the other one suggests and nods her head at the chair in front of the desk. I glance around the room as I go to sit, seeing the dated green rug and painted brown walls. There is nothing else in here other than the desk and chairs. The desk is covered in paperwork in neat piles and old cat statues that look out of place. There must be at least four cat statues that I can see with a quick glance, and their eyes seem to watch me like they know I hate them.

"I am Miss Ona, and this is my sister, Miss Noa. Welcome to Lost Time Academy. This must be a shock for you as it is for every descendant that walks through our doors," Miss Ona says with an almost kind smile.

"Not every day you wake up and find out all the fairy tales are real," I respond drily.

"No, it certainly is not," Miss Noa says, her tone sharper than her sisters.

"What fairy tale are you from then?" I ask.

"You may not understand the ways of our world, but let me inform you of something you would do well to remember. Asking what someone is, is considered *very* rude," Miss Noa snaps. Miss Ona shakes her head slightly at her sister's sharp reply but doesn't say a word to correct her or answer me. I don't say sorry, because I didn't know, nor do I think saying anything will benefit anyone right now.

"Now, your father sent word of your gifts, and you will be trained how to use them as well as your normal classes," Miss Ona says. The way they both speak, it's almost as if they are the same person; one finishes a sentence, and the next takes off after it perfectly.

"This is yours," Miss Noa says and slides a small book over to me. It has the symbol on the outside and my last name written in silver at the bottom. I open it up, seeing what looks like a blue cloud inside a mirror, and very slowly a face appears.

"Pleasure to meet you, Miss Dormiens," the face in the book says, and I scream, dropping it and jumping off my chair. *A talking bloody book.*

"That never gets old. It is always so funny," Miss Ona states, laughing, and I look up to see Miss Noa's lip twitch a little.

"That was mean, and it hurt," the book says, drawing my attention back to the book on the floor. The actual book is talking and being almost sarcastic. A sarcastic talking book. *This just gets better and better.*

"This is your family book. It will guide you to your classes, living quarters, and will answer any questions you may have about your powers and new school," Miss Ona tells me as I stare at the book on the floor like it is about to attack me or something.

"It talks," I respond in shock. "The book talks."

"Yes, Miss Dormiens. Do pick it up now. The

poor book is alive and does not like being left on the floor like a non-magical object," Miss Noa says in an unimpressed tone. I briefly look up, meeting her dark purple eyes, which are darker than her sisters, before walking over and picking up the book. The face in the book just glares at me like I wasn't meant to be shocked it talked.

"You may leave now, and your book will guide you to your room," Miss Ona says in a final tone.

"Fine. Thanks for your help, I suppose," I respond, smiling at them before walking away.

"One other thing, Miss Dormiens," Miss Noa's voice stops me as I get to the door.

"Yes?" I ask, pulling my gaze away from the weird book and the head staring at me still.

"Communication with anyone outside Lost Time Island is forbidden. We allow you to speak only to your parents once a week with our communications that are not human made. So do you have a phone or anything you wish to hand over now?" she asks me.

"No," I answer straightaway, feeling like the phone in my bag is burning a hole through my clothes, but I know it's not. I won't give up my only chance to talk to Quinton, even if he hates me for leaving him. I can't just stop all contact with him, no matter what I told my parents.

"If you are caught contacting anyone in the outside world, the repercussions would not be favourable," Miss Noa warns. I don't look back as I open the door and walk out without saying a word. I don't care what the repercussions are, I *won't* lose my only way to contact Quinton.

Chapter 4

"*N*ow take a right here," the head says, and I look up from the book to see where I'm walking. The book has led me up the stairs to what can only be described as a corridor-filled maze awaiting me. It's just dark corridor after other dark corridor, full of dead ends, and the book does *not* know its way. I know it is just as lost as I am. I can't believe I haven't seen one person on all these trips, so I can't ask for directions or how to get a better book tour guide. The lights are so dim as we get to another dead end, and I glare at the head in the book.

"Sorry, go back and walk down the corridor again. I am sure I know the way this time!" he exclaims with excited eyes. I do as he asks, even though I can't really see where I'm walking anyway.

I'm trusting a talking book to show me the way. *A talking book.*

"What's your name?" I ask the head floating in the book as we get back to the stairs where we started from in the first place. The head is shaved of all hair, but I can tell he is a guy from his male features and voice. The man has strange, grey, big, bright eyes and a small face which is kinda cute. I can see a sort of neck attached to the head, but then it's just blue clouds around everything else.

"Your ancestor used to call me Lane," Lane says, and I nod.

"You knew my ancestor?" I ask him.

"Yes. Each book belongs to a family, and only when a descendant gets their powers do I wake up. Let me tell you now, being asleep for a thousand years is not what I consider fun," he says, with almost a pout that's hard not to laugh at. "I'm sure the world has changed over time. For example, your hair is almost wild. Is that normal?"

"Kinda normal these days. So, Lane, how do you know where to go now?" I ask, wondering if he is just leading me around in circles, because it sure feels that way.

"Magic, little one. I'm a little rusty, but it's all coming back to me now!" he says with a grin. "In no time, we will be best friends, and I will find this room for you!"

"I'm not little by the way," I respond as I keep walking down the long corridor he promises my room is in.

"No, you're right, you do have unusually shaped big eyes and a large head," he nods in agreement, while I feel kind of insulted by that statement.

"I do not have a big head or eyes!" I exclaim as I stop walking to glare down at Lane.

"Maybe it's just my angle," he says nervously, coughing. If I could see his shoulders, then I would imagine him shrugging right now as well.

"Your room is three doors down," Lane says. "You nearly found it on your own. See? Team-work!" I laugh at his idea of teamwork. It was more luck than anything else. I keep walking past the doors on the right before getting to the third one like he suggested. I open the door knob and push the door open to a dark room. Thank god it wasn't locked.

"The light switch is on the wall behind the door," Lane tells me quietly, so quiet I almost miss his voice.

"Why is it behind the door? That's not a smart place to put it," I mutter before shutting the door. I suddenly feel a hand slide around my throat before someone slams me headfirst into the wall with her other hand. I blink as the person turns the light on but keeps her hand on my neck.

"Get the fuck off me!" I shout and freeze as I feel something cold and sharp pressed into my back. I don't move or try to fight whoever it is anymore, they have me stuck.

"Who are you?" the female voice comes behind me, but it's Lane that answers.

"Miss Dormiens is your new roommate, and violence out of fighting class is against the school's rules," Lane says, tutting.

"Shit," the girl mutters as she lets me go, and I gasp for air, my hand going to my throat the moment I am free. I turn with a glare to see my apparent roommate standing with her hands on her hips, glaring at me like I am the problem in this situation. The girl is about my age, with long blonde hair that is nearly as pale as her skin. She is a little shorter than I am, which is saying something as I'm not exactly tall myself. Her voice sounds American, but I'm not sure exactly where she is from, it's not a south accent.

"Sorry about that. I didn't know and thought… well, I thought you had broken in or something. The girls in this school can be bitches," she states, losing the glare as her bright turquoise green eyes lock onto me, and she offers me a hand, with the other one holding the sharp dagger. I look at her hand for a second, deciding whether to reject it or not. I mean, I get her point. In her mind, I snuck into her room and scared the crap out of her in the middle of the night. In some ways, I respect her spunk. "I'm Octavia, but call me Tavvy," she says as I shake her hand.

"I'm Madilynn, but my friends call me Madi. Thanks for the warning about the girls around here," I reply and let go of her hand to pick up the book off the floor. I raise my eyebrows down at him as I realise something.

"Did you know I had a roommate?" I ask Lane, who looks down at the blue cloud and not at me.

"Yes, but how would I know that the fairy descendant was anything other than sweet. I remember her ancestor being lovely and not having a stabby habit," Lane says with almost a guilty look as he avoids my eyes still.

"You still should have told me. I could have simply knocked on the door and avoided all this," I state, glaring down at him as he still won't look my way. I sigh and slowly close the book, noticing that he doesn't look at me once. I look over at Tavvy who slides the dagger under her pillow. Clearly, she sleeps with it for protection. *What kind of school have I just walked into?*

"So you're a descendant of fairies? Like Tinkerbell? The one in love with Peter Pan?" I ask once I put the book on the small table by the door, and she nods.

"Yep, I'm a fairy and all that, but I don't have my wings yet. Also, Peter Pan's descendant is a strange kid who can transform into a tree, so he never has to grow up. Not really my type. He is literally still twelve…and has been for hundreds of years. The tree is behind the castle. What are you?" she asks after blurting a crap load of information out about another descendant.

"Sleeping Beauty," I say, and Tavvy rolls her eyes.

"Another princess this year. I should have figured it out, you're beautiful," she says with a little shrug.

"I'm not—" I go to disagree with her, and she interrupts by placing her hand in the air.

"Don't try that one. All descendants who were made pretty in Disney films are fucking stunning in real life. You should see Cinderella's descendant, he is yummy…but also an asshole," she says, making me laugh a little. I already like my new roommate, I think.

"Is he?" I ask.

"Yep, all blond hair and crystal blue eyes, but he has issues with his powers, like all of us do," she sighs.

"What would Cinderella's descendant even get for powers? A fairy godmother?" I ask, thinking of the fairy tale and not knowing what else to imagine. She laughs before answering.

"Listen, most fairy tales the humans wrote... well, they got it wrong or mixed up. Cinderella could start fires, control them, and charm the opposite sex into falling for her," she explains to me, and it kind of makes sense in a weird way.

"Like the prince who fell for a servant," I muse.

"Exactly," she says with a grin. I wonder how different my own fairy tale is from the one I grew up reading and the Disney films I've watched. "Let me help you set the bed up," she offers, and I finally look around my room. The room has a bunk bed in the corner. The bottom bed is empty, and the top one is clearly Tavvy's with the pink sheets. There are two wardrobes and a large dressing table which is covered in stuff near the window. The one big window is concealed by black curtains, and there's not much else to look at. The walls have cracks in them, I notice, and it's not dusty, but it feels like an old room.

"You don't have to help. I woke you up, you should go back to sleep," I suggest, but she shakes her head.

"Nope, I want to help. I was alone when I got here, and it sucks not having a clue about anything. So the bathrooms are at the end of the corridor. Luckily, there is only one other girl who uses that bathroom as everyone is scared of the—" she starts to tell me and stops. "Never mind." I take my bag off my shoulder, wondering what exactly is scary about the bathroom and deciding to just leave it for tonight. I open my bag up, digging around for my red and cream bedsheets and silver blanket. I find them, and Tavvy makes the quilt while I sort the bottom sheet out.

"So red is your colour? I'm more a pink girl."

"I didn't choose these sheets actually. My mum bought them in case I got powers," I explain, smoothing down the sheet, "though the blanket is mine."

"It's not too bad. She could have picked worse," Tavvy replies, winking at me as she chucks the finished quilt my way. "I only started here two months ago when I got my powers. So we are in the same year, and luckily for you, I bet the same class- es," she tells me as I put my quilt on my bed. I'm happy to know someone at least for my first day tomorrow.

"Awesome," I eventually say, sliding off my coat after the bed is done, and pulling out my phone from my bag.

"They are serious about technology and how it's banned here. I'm just warning you, as a friend, that you should hide that," she says as I slide the phone inside the pillow case she hands me off the floor before putting the pillow on the bed.

"I know, but there is someone I need to stay in contact with, secretly at least…and he is worth the risk," I say, sitting on the bed, and she sits next to me. "Even if I can't actually tell him anything truthful, I just want to hear his voice."

"A boyfriend?" she asks, wagging her eyebrows.

"An ex-boyfriend now," I reply, trying to keep my voice from catching, and she gives me a sad smile.

"What's his name?" she gently asks me.

"Quinton," I reply with a tight smile.

"A sexy name, but I'm guessing he is human?" she asks, and I nod.

"Don't fall for a human," she says softly, and I laugh humourlessly.

"It's too late for that. I love him already, but it's clearly not meant to be between us now," I say.

"How long were you together?" she asks me, seeming curious now.

"About a year. We grew up together, well, him, me and the four other boys that lived on my street. When the others moved away three years ago, it was just us left, and I can't lose him now," I say.

"Okay Madi, but as long as he is just a friend now, it won't be a problem. I don't want you hurt, even if we did just meet. I'm sure your parents told you about the arranged marriage thing," she says, her eyes hold a note of worry.

"I know...but I didn't choose this. I didn't choose to walk away from Quinton, and I need to know he is okay. I need to know he is going to move on and have a life, even if it isn't the one we planned together," I whisper, harshly wiping my eyes. "Sorry, we just met, and I'm blurting out my depressing life issues."

"Hey, I get it, Madi. We have all left people behind back home. Look, they have trackers on 24/7 for phones. If you want to use it, go to the roof; it's the only place that would be safe, and it is difficult to get up there, so they don't check it. I'm sure your book will help you find a way up," she says, and I smile, thankful for her advice.

"Thank you, Tavvy. Any other advice I need to know before I go to sleep?" I ask her, desperate to change the subject now because it damn well hurts to talk about Quinton.

"Just one thing. There are four brothers here that unofficially rule the academy. The girls that follow them around will do *anything* to get their attention. They will make it their mission to destroy you if you mess with the brothers, so it's best to stay out of their way," she suggests, "though I'm not too worried, considering you just got out of a relationship. Everyone is waiting to hear who they are going to be arranged to marry. Their last fiancé died recently."

"Yeah, I'm not looking for anyone right now, and I'm sorry someone died... So, what's so special about the brothers anyway?" I ask her. She doesn't need to worry, no one will remotely interest me, not so soon after leaving Quinton.

"They are hot, for one, and extremely powerful. They basically rule the school, and even the teachers are scared of them," she says. "There are rules for us, and rules for them."

"They sound like assholes," I mutter, yawning. It's been a long ass day.

"They are, but I wouldn't go calling them that. One of them is super creepy, and he can pull you into another dimension he made as a kid. Everyone is scared of him, and he always wins fight class.

Well, except his brothers who can beat him when they feel like it," she chuckles. "Either way, it's best to stay clear."

"Then you have nothing to worry about. I will stay away from Mr. Creepy," I say, and she laughs. She climbs up the ladder and into her bed, still chuckling as I give her a confused expression.

"You haven't seen them yet. I bet your attitude might change."

Chapter 5

"Your first class is history," Lane says as I finish brushing my hair and look over at the open book on my bed. I pull my black hoodie closer around me, hoping that my casual skinny jeans and shirt is the right dress code. Though looking at Tavvy just behind me, I'm guessing it is fine. I don't know why anyone is worried about the bathroom down the corridor. I went this morning to use the toilet and freshen up with Tavvy, and there was nothing but a slightly old-fashioned bathroom.

"History is the worst class. You should have gotten here yesterday; the first class was Drama where they spend the year teaching you how to act if a human sees your powers. It's the best class," Tavvy says as she pulls on her leather jacket which matches her leather leggings she has on. I couldn't pull that outfit off if I tried, but Tavvy's skinny waist makes it work. I just threw on my comfy clothes with my trainers, and called it good enough. I've never been one to bother with what I'm wearing. I pull my hair up into a high ponytail as I watch Tavvy pick up a book like mine from the dressing table and open it.

"Morning, Tots! What are they serving for breakfast today?" she asks her book. I walk over, looking over Tavvy's shoulder at the woman's head in the book. She is bald like Lane and has blue eyes, with a triangle symbol on her cheek. You can only really tell she is a girl by her long eyelashes and high cheek bones. *What's with them all having no hair?*

"It is an English breakfast, your favourite. I believe today is the only day they are serving hot food for breakfast this week. So you might want to head over now before it is all eaten," she says, her voice is old-fashioned like Lane's too.

"Awesome," Tavvy states and shuts the book before putting it into her backpack. Once her bag is done up, she looks over at me and sighs before walking to the bed. "Here you go. I noticed you don't have one, and it's easier to carry things around," Tavvy explains as she leans under our beds and pulls out a black backpack.

"Thanks," I say and accept it, closing my book and putting it in the bag.

"Come on, new friend. Let's go before all the good food and seats are taken," Tavvy states and links her arm in mine, leading me out of our room. I'm surprised to see it's empty, and everywhere is very quiet when we walk out. This is meant to be a school...right?

"Where is everyone?" I ask her.

"There aren't that many students anymore, not like there used to be anyway. Not since...well, I'm sure someone will explain all that to you at some point. Overall, there are a hundred and fifty students, well, a hundred and fifty-one now," she says, knocking my shoulder as we walk down the very long corridor, and I frown at her.

"Explain what?" I ask her.

"About the dark fairy tale descendants and why there are so few of us left...I will explain tonight if you really want to know and not get any sleep for a while," she says, and smiles sadly at me. I nod once at her and remind myself to ask her about it all later. As I look around, I'm happy to say the place doesn't look as creepy in the day as it does at night. There is still a silly amount of old paintings of people, and now that I can see, there is lavender wallpaper that is horrible.

"There are only two other students that have a room down here," she explains to me, "though they are always late to class."

"There are ten doors," I comment, looking around as we come into the corridor that joins all the corridors going off it. The stairs going down are in the middle of the corridor, and the stairs going up are next to them. The old and derelict feel of the mansion is the same up here too, and more strange paintings line the walls.

"Yep, each corridor has ten rooms. The floor upstairs is the boys' rooms, which is a maze of corridors as well. We aren't allowed up there, but that doesn't stop *some* people," she nods her head to the red-haired girl walking down the stairs, dressed in a small red dress and killer black heels. She stops when she sees us, taking her time to look us up and down before walking over, her heels clanging loudly against the floor.

"The new girl everyone is talking about," she states when she stops in front of us, raising a black eyebrow.

"Err yeah. Hi," I say with an awkward wave, and she wrinkles her nose as she looks me over again.

"When you want to learn how to dress, come and find me," she states. Rude.

"No, thanks," I reply, and she laughs, wrapping her hand around my upper arm as she leans in close.

"Lose the fake fairy, sweetheart, and come and play with the ones who have actual power and can keep you alive," she taunts, and I pull my arm away from her.

"*Fake fairy?* Do you want to say that again?" Tavvy basically growls, and her skin starts glittering green. There is actual green glitter appearing all over her, and green dust falls to the floor. Holy Batman, that is cool.

"What are you going to do, sprinkle fairy dust on me?" the read head laughs, and I put my hand on Tavvy's shoulder, making her look at me.

"Whoever this typical high school bitch is, she isn't worth it," I tell Tavvy, whose green sparkling eyes freak me out for a second before she sighs and nods. The sound of footsteps drift to us just before three teenage guys around my age come down the stairs, and we all look over at them. They curiously watch us, or rather me, before walking away as more people start coming out their rooms, and the corridor quickly fills up.

"Another time, fake fairy," the redhead says before walking off, and both Tavvy and I watch her silently until she is gone down our corridor. So that must be one of our corridor roommates.

"That bitch was one of the ones I warned you about last night, her name is Ella," Tavvy says, shaking the dust off her so it falls into a puddle at her feet.

"I know it's rude to ask, but what fairy tale is she from?" I ask.

"You know the Little Mermaid? Well, she is her descendant. Ella is a killer in the water and with her family's trident. She can also become a mermaid at will and heal herself and others with water," Tavvy explains to me.

"Doesn't sound something to be scared of," I admit.

"No, she is useless on land with no water nearby. Though she has been trained her whole life to fight, like most of us have, and could kill you in a second," she explains.

"You've been trained?" I ask as she links our arms again, and we start walking towards the stairs.

"You haven't?" she asks, and I sigh. So it seems I'm at a major disadvantage here.

"Erm no," I reply. Why wouldn't my parents teach me how to fight if everyone else was taught?

"Well, fighting class is all day Friday, and they

take it super seriously. It's like sixty percent of your year grade. You have to win or at least be able to keep yourself awake for most the day," she warns me, and I just mentally groan because there is nothing I can say out loud to that. Nearing the bottom of the stairs, we both pause in the middle of the steps when we hear a loud bang coming from just outside the doors. Seconds later, the doors are blasted open, and a man goes flying through them, sliding across the floor. I cover my face with my hands as dust from the broken door flies at us, and then when the dust clears, I see three men walking through the doorway.

Each one of them is stood next to each other, their faces so familiar that it hurts when their shocked gazes meet mine. They are the very last people I expected to see here. When I pull my gaze away to the man on top of the door on the floor, his familiar brown eyes meet mine.

"Madilynn, is that you?"

Chapter 6

N *oah, Knox, Tobias and Oisin.*

"Shit," the guys say in unison as I cautiously step down the stairs until I'm stood right over Noah. He looks up at me, and his eyes widen in clear shock as he wipes blood off his cut lip. I haven't seen him in so long, and I can't stop myself from just gaping at him.

"Madi?" he asks me again. I try to shake off my shock, watching as he stands up off the door and wipes the dust off his torn shirt. The boy I remember is long gone, and in his place is a guy with giant muscles, handsome strong features and soft brown hair that is shaved short yet looks incredibly sexy. If it weren't for those light brown eyes I never forgot, I would hardly recognise the boy I grew up with.

"Noah?" I ask, not even trying to mask my shocked tone at seeing him. I turn and look at the others who watch me from the doorway. Again, none of them look like the boys I remember... except for their eyes and the way they look at me like I belong to them. *I always did...until they left me.* I can't get over how different they all look, nothing like the boys I remember. Tobias, Knox and Oisin stand still in surprise, their eyes locked onto me with expressions I can't read past the shock. All three of them scream power and strength now, the geeky boys I remember seeming lost. It's the look they give me, and I know everything has changed but that one look.

"She changes *nothing*," Tobias snaps, his angry gaze meeting mine briefly before he turns and walks out the doorway where the door was once being held. Tobias was always the quiet one of the bunch. *What the hell happened to him?*

"You guys are still fighting, I see. Is it still over who gets to play on the computer first?" I sarcastically ask, and Noah laughs as I try to smile back at him, but it's a tense and tight smile at best. I can't help how betrayed I feel. They left me by choice all those years ago...and I was heartbroken back then. They all must be fairy descendants to be here, and not one of them seems to know what to say as I look them all over. Oisin just runs his hands through his wavy blond hair as he stares at me, his light silver eyes just as playful as I remember. I turn my gaze to Knox who has his massive muscular arms crossed, his dark silver eyes narrowed on me and still as serious as always. I used to play a game where the goal would be to make Knox smile or laugh, and I have a feeling those games won't work on the guy staring at me like I'm the cause of all his problems now.

"Oh my god, you know the Tale brothers?" Tavvy harshly whispers, shaking me out of my staring, and I look back at her and nod.

"We grew up together, but I haven't seen any of them in three years because they left," I say, my words making some of them flinch a little.

"I can't believe you're here," Noah says, stepping closer to me and then pulling me into a tight hug. When I wrap my arms around him in return, I can feel the difference in his body since I last hugged him. He feels like all muscle. He smells the same though, like honey. I always loved how Noah smelt, and I used to steal his shirts to sleep in. I still have one in my bag upstairs...and the thought makes my cheeks light up a little.

"Why am I not surprised the Tale brothers are the cause of the mess here? All of you, in my office now!" Miss Noa's sharp voice comes from behind me. Noah lets me go, running his hands down my arms as I hear Oisin reply to Miss Noa.

"The door fell off on its own. What did you want us to do about it? This place is falling apart," he says, the lie smooth from his lips, and if I didn't know the truth, I would almost believe him. I frown at his lie, and he seems to sense me looking his way as he turns his head to grin at me.

"So if I touch this door and use my gift to see the past, I'm just going to see a door falling?" Miss Noa asks as she crosses her arms, and Oisin laughs.

"Fine, fine. We broke the door, but give me a minute before you tell us off," he says as he holds up his hands in surrender, before coming over to me as Miss Noa protests. But I don't hear her words as I stare at Oisin. He was always very attractive; he just had this thing about him that any girl would have trouble ignoring. Oisin has pure gold blond hair and matching tanned skin, but now everything is so much...well, more than I remember him being. He looks like he stepped out of an advert off the television. Everything about him is alluring.

"Nice to see you again, Sleepy. You have changed one hell of a lot," he says and lifts my hand, pressing a kiss to the back of it, and I raise my eyebrows at him. *What's with the flirting?*

"Sin, come on, man. We are already in the shit because you couldn't keep your mouth shut," Knox shouts over, and he briefly looks at me before walking off.

"Sin?" I ask Oisin, not remembering that nickname as kids. I always just called him Oisin, like the others did.

"Just like your nickname, Sleepy—it's what I'm good at." He winks, making me blush before walking off after Knox, and Noah follows him, with only a brief look back at me.

"You have some explaining to do," Tavvy suggests as she walks over to me. I look at the broken door and think about how strong Tobias must have been to knock the door down by throwing Noah. *Crazy strong.* What's more concerning is how Noah only looked a little winded by being thrown through a door, not knocked out like he should have been.

"Let me guess, they are the powerful students you told me to stay away from?" I ask, and she gives me a sympathetic look.

"Let's get some food, and we can chat," she says and walks off, with me following. My parents always said to stay away from the Tale brothers…*maybe they had a point.*

Chapter 7

"Well, out with it…how do you know them then?" Tavvy asks once we sit down with our trays of food on one of the benches outside. There are a few strange-looking students sat around, but I can't focus on them as my mind keeps picturing the guys over and over. I see the geeky boys who used to chase me down the street in a race to see who could get to the ice cream van first. I think back to the last time I saw them…and how it broke me for a long time. Quinton loved them like brothers as well…we were both crushed when they left.

"Shh, keep it down! My parents might hear you!" I whisper

as I try not to laugh as Tobias falls through my window, his lanky body too big for the tiny window.

"It was a lot easier to sneak in when I was younger," Tobias huffs, glaring at the window as he sits up off the floor and grins over at me as I keep laughing.

"Whatever, loser. Get in here," Quinton says from where he is sat on my bed. Quinton has had a growth spurt recently, and the once skinny boy is now quite bulky, with wide shoulders and a six pack I spotted a few days ago when he had his shirt off as he mowed the lawn for my mum. All the neighbours paid him to mow their lawns after seeing him doing mum's.

"Where are Oisin, Noah and Knox?" I ask when no one else comes through the window after a while, because I thought they were coming here tonight as well. We always meet up on Saturdays at one of our houses to hang out. It's almost like a ritual now.

"I just wanted to see you, speak to you before…" he pauses and rubs the back of his head. When Tobias walks past me to sit next to Quinton, I'm shocked how he is so much taller than Quinton even now. Tobias and his twin brother, Noah, are the same age as Quinton and me. His twin brothers, Knox and Oisin, are a few months older. His parents adopted them not long after Knox and Oisin's parents, who were best friends with Tobias and Noah's parents, died suddenly. Even though they aren't blood related, they are brothers in every sense. Quinton is like the brother they adopted at some point, and I

suppose I'm like their sister who they can't get rid of if they tried.

"Before what?" I ask quietly. Each one of the boys have been acting weird this week...maybe that has something to do with it.

"Nothing. Knox, Noah and Oisin aren't coming tonight. Mum and dad needed them for something," he mutters, not really giving me an answer. When his eyes meet mine, I know he wants me to forget it.

"Alright. Nothing serious though?" I have to ask him.

"Nope. Now come here," Tobias suggests, patting the space on the bed between him and Quinton. I walk over and sit between them, and we all lie back, looking up at the white ceiling. I try to ignore how different it has been feeling to be close to Tobias and Quinton and the others recently. Every time they touch me makes my cheeks burn red like they are starting to now.

"You remember what we all agreed on mine and Noah's eleventh birthday?" Tobias asks Quinton and me as I turn my head to look at him. Seeing how serious he is makes me pause. Quinton answers before I do.

"That we would protect each other, always."

"Remember that, Sleepy," Tobias tells me firmly. "Always."

*T*hey didn't even say goodbye, not really. That was the last time I saw any of them. The next Monday, they didn't turn up for school, and when I went to their house after to check on them, it was empty. The neighbour told me they had all moved out and left the village yesterday. I don't even remember walking to Quinton's and crying for the next week. Eventually, the sadness turned into anger that they didn't even say goodbye.

Now that anger is just shock and confusion. They are descendants like me…maybe that is why they left, but then that doesn't make any sense. If everyone is given the book on their seventeenth birthday, they couldn't have left to come here when they were fifteen. My birthday is the latest in the year out of all of us, except for Quinton whose birthday is next week. It hurts that I'm not going to be celebrating it with him, and he is going to be alone.

"Madi…you okay?"

I shake my head and focus on Tavvy, knowing that I can't change anything. "We all lived on the same street. All of them, me and Quinton."

"I guess their parents wanted them to grow up around a female descendant from a powerful line,"

Tavvy muses. "Unlucky that they chose you. The Tale brothers are not who you want to know around here."

"Why would their parents want us to grow up together?" I ask her as I eat some toast after dipping it in my beans.

"Females are rarer for us, especially ones with descendant powers. The male to female ratio is way off. I think there are only twenty girls here and a hundred and thirty guys," she says, and I look around. She is right, there is all guys here, and I can't see another girl in sight.

"My parents told me they marry off people here. So how does that work if there are so many guys?" I ask, curious about it. *Do some people just not marry? As I want to sign up for that.*

"They didn't explain that they usually choose four to five guys for one girl? It used to be two guys until about thirty years ago when they decided to propose more males to one female," she says, and my eyes widen in shock. An arranged marriage to five guys? I don't even see how it could work. Wouldn't there be jealousy? It was difficult having five male friends growing up, but luckily, they never treated me like more than a friend...except for a few times in secret.

"No, they didn't mention that," I say, not knowing what else to say.

"It's not that bad, don't look so terrified," she chuckles. "The male descendants look like gods around here. Five god-looking guys worshipping your every move…it isn't that bad."

"Right, but how would one girl even keep up with five guys?"

"I don't know, but I am looking forward to finding out," she winks, and to my surprise, I laugh.

"Wait, even if they did that, there aren't enough females here for the males," I say, doing the math in my head.

"Yeah, that's true, but when you take off the twenty percent that join the Masters' army, and then the rest are married off to the descendants that didn't get powers," she says. "Only weak descendants get married off to non-powers."

"What is the Masters' army?" I ask, my confused look just makes her sigh a little, but she does tell me.

"They fight the dark fairy tales that love to kill us. Look, you're going to learn a lot today and not one bit of it is going to be good, but I'll tell you one thing," she says.

"What?" I ask.

"I'll be there, and at least you will have a friend

in this hell hole. I never had that," she says, smiling at me. "Life as a descendant isn't easy or safe without friends."

"Are we safe here? From the dark fairy tales?" I ask quietly, because I feel anything but safe in this academy.

"For now, Madi. They are getting stronger, and that's why you need to learn everything you can here," she says and carries on eating her food in silence. I pick at my food, waiting for her to finish her food and wondering how dangerous it actually is in this world I've been thrown into.

Chapter 8

"*P*lease take a seat over there, and it's lovely to meet you, Miss Dormiens," the teacher says when I walk in the room, following Tavvy closely. This whole place is a complete maze, and I couldn't be more thankful for Tavvy right now. The teacher doesn't seem surprised to have a new student, though when I think about it, she must have new students turn up all the time. The teacher looks about seventy, with a wrinkled face, grey hair up in a bun, and a long yellow dress on with a brown belt around her waist.

"Hi, it's nice to meet you too," I reply to her with a smile, and she nods with a strange look. I quickly pull my gaze away and shut the door behind me before looking around the classroom. The class only has ten people in it, all guys, and my eyes catch Noah's straightaway as he sits at the back of the classroom, spinning a pencil on his desk. Noah never used to be able to sit still when we were younger, and it seems like that hasn't changed at least. I wonder what fairy tale he is from; his looks don't give me any clue. Noah just looks like your typical hot boy next door, but it is clear he isn't exactly normal. No one in this room is.

"Here," Noah says as I walk further in the room, reaching a hand out to hold out a seat next to him. I look over at Tavvy who sits at the desk nearer the front of the class, who has empty seats next to her. I mouth "sorry" to an annoyed looking Noah before going to sit next to Tavvy instead.

"You chose me over the hottie," Tavvy says, flashing a surprised smile my way.

"The hottie knows where I am if he wants to move," I reply, shrugging a shoulder as I take my bag off and push it under the desk.

"You think I'm hot?" Noah asks, making me jump a little, and a few guys in the room laugh around us. Noah pulls out the seat next to me and sits down, pushing his bag under his seat next to mine before focusing all his attention on me.

"Only a little bit hot," I reply, making his lips twitch.

"I'm offended. I was your first kiss, and I'm only

a little bit hot?" he says, reminding me of the time we decided to practice kissing because everyone at school was doing it.

"We were eleven, it hardly counts. None of us knew what we were doing," I say, ignoring how he leans close, so close I can feel his warm breath across my own lips when I turn to look at him.

"Should we practise kissing again? I will make sure it counts, Madi," he whispers seductively in a way that I'm sure most girls would fall for.

"If we follow that rule, I'll have to kiss you all. As I remember having *five* first kisses," I whisper back, and he grins in a teasing way.

"Touché, Sleepy," he chuckles, crossing his arms and leaning back in his seat, making me feel like I can breathe again.

"I see you haven't changed all that much since we were kids. You always teased me with things back then," I reply, and he nods.

"Though I'm better at it now. How is Quinton?" he asks me, but I don't get to answer him even though him just mentioning Quinton makes my heart ache and the smile on my lips disappear.

"So, class, we have a new student. Everyone, this is Miss Dormiens, and I'm Miss Cata," she says, and I look away from Noah, thankful for the distraction. What could I tell Noah anyway? That I left Quinton just like they all did? That he is alone, and I miss him so much? "As we have a new student, I believe it would be best to have a refresher class on the very basics of our history. It will be good to see if any of you were listening," she says, and there are several groans from other students around the room.

"Great. She does this every time someone new comes here," Tavvy mutters next to me, crossing her arms and resting back.

"Who wants to go first?" Miss Cata asks, and most of the class sinks down further in their seats. Noah puts his hand up, and Miss Cata nods for him to speak.

"There are good and evil descendants, just like there are good and bad humans. We are descendants of the good fairy tales' characters, though the villains in our stories are what are known as dark fairy tales. Every one of us has a dark fairy tale enemy whose powers can destroy us. Just like our powers can destroy them," he says, and Miss Cata nods. In my fairy tale, there was an evil fairy who could transform into a dragon. That doesn't sound good.

"Yes, and that is why the Masters' army was created. The Masters' army fights them every day to keep ourselves and humans safe. The Masters' army is free for any descendants to join, but there are rules for joining. Does anyone want to say them?" she asks, and a guy near the front puts his hand up.

"Relationships are forbidden, you cannot leave once you have joined. The only way to leave the army is death or a great honour. Once you enlist in the Masters' army, the army protects you no matter what, and you do whatever they tell you to do or face death," the guy solemnly says. *That sounds like a crap deal.*

"Yes, all correct. Now can anyone tell me about the Masters themselves?" she asks, and another guy puts his hand up and leans back in his seat before he starts talking.

"The Masters are a group of five descendants from the strongest lines. The Masters control the army, the homes, the schools and everything we need to stay safe in our lives. Each Master has a council of five trusted descendants, and they pass judgement on everything in our community," the guy explains, looking over at me for a second, and I smile at him. Something seems to spook him as he quickly looks away. I glance over at Noah who has his arms crossed, watching the teacher with a smirk on his lips. Strange.

"Very good. As most of you know, the Masters

took control over two hundred years ago to stop the ongoing war between our races. Only, the dark ones didn't want to stop the war, so the Masters ended up protecting us instead with a united front. They are the most powerful of our race, and their children will take their places when they retire at the age of fifty," she says, looking over at us for a second before looking away. "Now everyone come and get a book from the front and continue reading for the next hour. I expect you to take notes because you will be tested on this. Miss Dormiens, you need to catch up, so you are expected to do reading in your personal hours. For now, start at the beginning."

"That sounds like a lot of work," I groan, meaning to say it quietly, but everyone hears, and there are a few snickers as Miss Cata narrows her eyes at me.

"I have every belief that you will catch up shortly," she replies and claps her hands. "Come on, we do not have all day." I quickly get up at the same time as everyone else and grab a book off the front desk before returning to my seat. I open the book to the first page, noticing how Noah and Tavvy open theirs to somewhere in the middle of the book before I start to read.

The book starts off with explaining how descendants hid their powers from the humans by magically blessing islands off the coast of Ireland, and over the years, the humans forgot the islands existed. The islands cannot be found by a human anymore, therefore they are a safe place for our kind to live. Most descendants choose to bring their children up off the island so they can have a normal life, but if a child is brought up on the island, they can be told about their heritage early. I frown when a ripped piece of paper is slid onto the page in my book, and I look up, checking the teacher isn't looking before unfolding it.

Skip the next class with me? I want to spend some time with you. Alone. -Noah.

I look over at him and shake my head when he smirks at me. I'm not skipping any classes on my first day. I slide the note into my pocket before going back to reading about how the dark fairy tale descendants have their own island. I look over as Noah rips another piece of paper off a notebook he has on his table and quickly writes something on it. He grins at me as he slides it onto my book again. I roll my eyes at him before opening the note.

You have health class next. Everyone skips it. Come with me, Sleepy. I know you have a million questions buzzing around in that pretty head of yours. -Noah

"Go with him, I will cover you. He is right, no one bothers with that class. Most seventeen-year-olds know about sex and how to have a baby by now. They only make us go to the class to make sure we girls understand the basics and repopulate. It's gross," Tavvy whispers to me, and I turn to see her looking over at the note. She winks at my low chuckle and hands me a pen. I quickly scribble on the note and pass it back to Noah. I watch him open it, and I bite my lip when he grins at me before sliding the note into his pocket. I look down at my book and try to read it instead of thinking about spending time alone with Noah Tale.

Chapter 9

*N*oah slides his arm around my shoulders after I say goodbye to Tavvy, who looks pleased with herself before walking off. I don't know what is going through her head about Noah and me, but I'm not encouraging her. I let Noah guide me down the corridors, towards the main hallway which is filled with students going to their lessons. Most stop to look at us or start whispering as they flash glances my way. I look over as I spot Ella with two blond guys at her side, all of them are stood with their arms crossed, watching us with serious expressions. I wave at Ella, who doesn't wave back, but instead she narrows her eyes at me.

"Ella is not someone to be friends with in here. She has been trying to get close to us since we moved to the island," Noah warns me, and I look up at him as we get to the doors at the end of the corridor he has led me down.

"You moved to the island? Is that where you all went?" I ask him as he lets me go to put his hand on the doorknob. I try to hide the pain in my voice, but I'm pretty sure he hears it anyway.

"Yeah, our parents moved us here and told us about our heritage early," he explains, flashing me a slightly sad look before looking away towards his hand. I gape as his hand glows bright yellow, and a burning smell drifts to me. When he moves his hand away and the glow is gone, I can see he has burnt a hole where the handle used to be, and he effortlessly pushes the door open.

"So, you glow? What is your descendant power?" I ask him as I walk into the glass house we have stepped into. Noah closes the door behind us, not answering me as I stare around the room. The greenhouse is huge, filled to the rim with multi-coloured plants and even some trees, by the looks of it. There is a yellow stone path down the middle that leads to a circle waterfall with brown benches all around it.

"My heritage is a little hard to explain, but let's go and sit before I tell you," he suggests, waving a hand at the benches. Purely because I want to know what his descendant power is, and just because I want to talk to him, I follow.

"I'm guessing you're something to do with light?" I ask, waiting to see.

"Close," he says, sitting right next to me and looking over at the water falling from the fairy statue's hands in the middle of the waterfall.

"Out with it then," I say, turning a little and running my finger over the water in the basin.

"Okay, so my family always has twins. Every single generation has had powers, no exception. Our line is close to the human's fairy tale of the sun and the moon. The human's fairy tale says a mother cursed her children because of how they acted. The one man was cursed to always burn and be hated. The daughter was blessed to be cool and loved. But I glow like the sun, literally, and Tobias glows like the moon. He freezes things though, not burns them like me," he explains, and I'm a little speechless for a moment.

"Okay, wasn't expecting that," I chuckle. I'm literally a little shocked.

"There is a rumour that the actual sun and moon where named after our ancestors, but who really knows?" he shrugs like it's no big deal. I get a sleeping princess, and he gets the freakin' sun. *Go figure.*

"It shouldn't shock me too much. You guys always did blow hot then cold with each other," I say thinking back to how Noah and Tobias were always arguing with each other. Tobias was the more playful one back then, but now, it seems the roles have reversed somehow. "And everyone else if I remember right."

"Not you though. Never our sleepy girl," he admits. "We *never* pushed you away."

"You left...none of you even bothered saying goodbye to me," I blurt out, though my voice is quiet, and I can't meet his eyes as I keep talking. "None of you said a word, and it crushed me. It crushed Quinton as well."

"Do you think we wanted to leave you? Fucking hell, we all fought as hard as we could to stay, Madi!" Noah snaps, and my eyes widen as all of Noah glows slightly yellow. Almost like a shimmer covers his skin, and suddenly, the room feels a lot warmer than it already was. I don't know what expression is on my face, but Noah growls in response, picking my hand up off the water, but I pull my hand out of his grasp and stand up.

"I only wanted a goodbye. *A reason.* Anything other than my best friends disappearing like I meant *nothing* to them," I tell him, finally meeting his eyes which are swimming with guilt. "You just left."

"You had Quinton," Noah retorts in anger, standing up. "We came back once…just to see you. You and Quinton looked happy enough together as you kissed in your room." I flinch at his accusation and how he knows Quinton and I were together.

"I love him as much as I loved each one of you…but he didn't leave me. Quinton stayed…" I snap back, my voice trailing off with more emotion than I wanted to admit to.

"Our parents are on the Masters' council. Our grandparents were before them, and my parents had to come back because of the war. We didn't have a choice in the decision," he tells me, and I finally look down at him. Noah isn't looking at me, his head bowed down, staring at the floor. "I wanted to stay."

"I missed you," I whisper in response, because that is what this all comes down to. I miss them all more than I ever thought I could miss someone. It seems messed up that I finally have them back in my life, only to lose Quinton because of it. I guess I never imagined a future where we would all be together, but I damn well hoped for it.

"We fucking missed you more, Sleepy. Every-thing went to shit the moment we left you," he whispers, rubbing his jaw with his hand and stepping closer.

"Since when do you and Tobias fight?" I ask.

"Tobias has issues. I—no, we all—were trying to stop him from messing up again," he explains. "The stuff he has gotten himself into will kill him or get him kicked off the island."

"What kind of things?" I ask quietly.

"Stuff I'm not worrying you with. Not when we just got you back," he says, stretching his arms above his head. I follow the movement with my eyes, eating up every muscle on his arms and how his golden skin is so smooth, it almost has a shine to it. I decide to leave what is going on with Tobias for now…I can ask him later. Or stalk him around the academy to find out. Someone will know, if the Tale brothers are as popular as Tavvy suggests they are.

"I did bring you here for another reason than to just skip class. I have to do a favour for some classmates," he says, offering me a hand. I don't pause as I slide my hand into his, enjoying how warm his hand is and letting him lead me around the fountain. We walk right to the back of the greenhouse where there is a row of plants in wooden plant pots. I look down to see all of them are growing well except for three of them. I watch as Noah lets go of my hand and walks to one of the dying plants. He places his hand just above it, and his hand glows lightly. *Warmly.* The plant slowly gets back its colour and grows gradually until it is bigger than the other plants, and it has little blue flowers blossoming from the edges.

"You can heal plants?" I ask him in wonder.

"Yep," he replies with a grin. "I can heal people and myself as well, it just hurts like a bitch." I laugh as he picks up some garden cutters off the side and cuts off one of the flowers. Noah walks over to me, and I freeze as he stops right in front of me.

"A late birthday present," he says, stroking the flower down my cheek slowly and making my mouth part a little. I reach for the flower, and he closes his hand around mine before leaning in and gently kissing my cheek. "It's good to have you back with us. You were always meant to be here because you're far more special than you know…but we all knew it the moment we met you."

Chapter 10

oah keeps his arm around my shoulders as we walk into the dining room for lunch, and we must be late to get here because everyone is sitting down with their food. Every pair of eyes seems to turn our way as we walk through the gap in the middle of the tables, towards the front of the room. Knox, Sin and Tobias all sit at one table, and the one next to it is where Ella is sat with her group of friends. I don't spot Tavvy anywhere in the room, not at the table we sat at from breakfast either, so I'm assuming she has skipped lunch today.

"Sit down, I will get you lunch. I still remember what you like to eat," Noah suggests when we get to the table where his brothers are sitting at.

"Thanks," I say, pulling a chair out next to Sin

and sitting down. Noah walks off, leaving me in the awkward silence of his brothers looking at me, but no one actually says a single word. Knox stares down at his food, eating away like I'm not here. Tobias is staring at me, completely silent which is stranger. Sin keeps parting his mouth like he wants to say something but doesn't know what. I feel that, because I don't know what to say to them. The silence just goes on until Noah brings back a tray of food and pulls the chair out next to me to sit down. I can't get over how different they all look now, so much older than I thought they would. I imagined how they would look many times, but this wasn't it. They are darker in nature, full of secrets that I wonder what it would take to make them tell me.

"Ham and cheese sandwiches, still your favourite, right?" Noah asks with a cheeky grin. "With salt and vinegar crisps, of course."

"Perfect," I say, taking my sandwich up off the plate as Noah digs into his. "Yours is a chicken club sandwich with cheese and onion crisps. Right?"

"Yep," Noah grins at me, clearly happy I remember. I remember everything about them. I could guess what Tobias, Knox and Sin are eating as well.

"How long did it take Quin to make a move

after we left?" Sin asks. "Quin is a dark horse, I'll give him that."

"You really want to know that?" I ask them all, because even though Sin asked, they might as well have all asked.

"Call me curious," Sin replies.

"A while. I always loved him, I just didn't know it until then," I answer them, not missing how each of them doesn't look pleased with the answer. If I was a smart girl, or any other girl in here, I wouldn't have been so honest.

"We had a pact, you know that?" Knox informs me, but I didn't have a clue.

"No. What was the pact?" I enquire.

"That we don't touch you. None of us. Quin was part of the pact, too, because he was a brother to us. Still is, though we can't tell him about this place and our world," Noah explains to me. Quin thought the same thing about them, he always did. We had each other, and nothing else mattered. Now Quin is alone, and I'm here with the brothers.

"Quin broke that pact then," I whisper, before taking a deep bite of my sandwich.

"It means there are no rules anymore. Does that scare you, Madi?" Sin asks. His voice is teasing, but I know Sin well enough to know he isn't joking one bit. They are all silent, watching me closely for the answer, because even if Sin is the brave one to ask first, they all want to know. We were best friends, closer than I am to even my family. They are my family, I always felt that way. Though as we grew older, it became more than anything we could have prepared for. I always wondered if that was the reason their parents took them away from me.

"No," I answer, knowing that the answer is so important to us all. Tobias pushes away from his table and walks away like he has done since he saw me this morning.

"Ignore him. He will come around soon," Knox says, watching Tobias walk away.

"Why is he mad?" I ask.

"Tobias fought the most not to leave you. Our parents had to lock him up for a month when we got here because he kept trying to leave. Give him time, because I tell you now, everything has gone to shit since we got here," Sin explains to me, and I sit in silence.

"Tavvy told me to stay away from you guys," I mutter, watching them. "That you are dangerous. Is that true? Have you changed that much that you are now dangerous?"

"She should tell everyone else that, but not you," Knox tells me, not seeming concerned at all about Tavvy's warnings.

"I hope not," I say, leaning back in my seat. I turn my gaze away from them to see everyone looking at us still, watching our every move—especially the girls, and one in particular, Ella. I might not need to worry about the brothers being dangerous, but Tavvy was right; it's the people that follow them who are dangerous.

Chapter 11

"Hey, new girl!" a voice shouts behind me just as I'm about to open the door to my room after Noah walked me back to the main corridor after dinner, a dinner at which Oisin and Knox sat with us. Tobias sat with us too, but he didn't say much to me. It was awkward as hell, and I have to find a way to talk to them alone, I think. Noah told me we would see each other tomorrow in class before he went up to his room. I look back to see Ella walking down the corridor towards me, her arms crossed tightly, matching her tense smile.

"Ella, right?" I say, leaning against the wall and waiting to see what crap she comes out with. I'm used to girls like her by now. Most of the pretty, popular girls at school always hated me because I was close to the only hot guys for miles. Some tried being my friend to get close. Others tried flat out being a bitch to me from the start and hated that I didn't care or listen to them. You get tough skin being friends with guys that most of the schoolgirls want to date. Though the guys did date some of them at times, it never lasted more than a week, and they never chose girls that tried to be a bitch to me or use me.

"Madi, right?" Ella mimics me, and I roll my eyes at her petty response. There isn't much chance of us being friends at this point. "Look, there is a party this weekend, and you should come." I almost laugh at her inviting me to a party. *Seriously?*

"Why the hell would you invite me?" I ask her, playing along for a moment.

"The Tale brothers have never come to a party here. Not once. If you go, so will they," she says. I raise my eyebrows in surprise. I didn't expect her to actually give me an honest answer rather than just lying and claiming she wants me to go as her friend. I somewhat respect her honest answer.

"Ah, I see. You're trying to use me to get to them," I muse. It's been done before.

"I heard you grew up together. You can't blame a girl for trying?" she replies, and to my surprise, I laugh. Ella hands me a white envelope about the size of my hand, and I sigh as I accept it.

"I will come—with Tavvy—but no promises the Tale brothers will follow me," I say. "I like parties with booze though. There will be booze, right?"

"Yeah, the pixie girls are making it. Trust me, the human stuff can't compare," she says, and I smile at her, forgetting for a moment she is using me and not actually being my friend. Ella straightens up, losing her smile before continuing with her reason for coming here. "None of the Tale brothers have even looked at a girl since they got here, but they watch you like a hawk. Even when you don't see it. They will come if you do."

"Fair warning, I think you need to find someone else to crush on," I warn her. "You are gorgeous and wasting your time."

"Is that a threat? Are you really claiming them all as yours?" she asks me.

"I never said that," I say, holding up my hands.

"Then until you tell me they are yours, they are fair game," she says with a grin. "I think I might actually like you, new girl." A brief flash of jealousy flitters through me as I watch her walk away and go into her room at the start of the corridor. I can't be jealous of someone liking the brothers. I mean, they can do whatever they want. *Whoever.* Even perfect red-haired mermaid girl. I shake my head as I walk into my room and see Tavvy sat on the window edge, reading a book with a woman covered in snow on the cover.

"Good time with Noah?" she asks, sitting up and closing the book.

"Sort of," I say, putting my bag down on the floor before going to sit on my bed. I pass her the envelope, and she accepts it, frowning down at it.

"It smells like the sea," she states. "Let me guess, mermaid girl gave you it?"

"We are invited to a party, apparently," I explain to her, leaving out that I kinda invited Tavvy to come with me. There is no way I am going alone. I open up the wardrobe where I put my clothes this morning and pull out my comfort hoodie, pulling it over my head and pulling up the hood.

"Ah, so she thinks being your friend will get her in the Tale brothers' pants," she says, laughing. "It makes sense in a messed up way, I suppose."

"Is it bad I got jealous at the idea of them being with her? I mean, I haven't even spoken with Tobias and Knox in three years. Noah is strange with me, and Oisin only spoke to me once at lunch," I say. "You were there, you saw how awkward it was."

"It's not bad. Complicated maybe? Sure. Though the Tale brothers could have slept with most of the girls in the school by now if they wanted to, but they don't fuck around or even seem interested. I always thought there must be a girl who stole their hearts first, and then I saw how they looked at you," she says, and I shake my head at her.

"They don't like me that way," I explain to her. "I'm more like a little sister to them."

"Totally clueless," she says, laughing her head off as I glare at her. She tuts at me as she opens the envelope in her hands. I jump back as dozens of mini paper butterflies explode out of the envelope before flying into a key shape, moulding together until the key drops to the floor.

"Urgh, how tacky. The nymph twins must have been helping her make the invites. They specialise in making flying and glittery stuff that annoys everyone," she says, pulling the letter out of the envelope while I go and pick up the white key.

"The key is entrance to the party. It is being held in the attic which is perfect for you to sneak off to the roof and call your human lover boy," she says, putting the letter on top of her book and dropping it on the desk. "I've never been to one of their parties, but the wards make sure the teachers don't know it is happening."

"Well, you are going with me and keeping me from throwing something at the mermaid chick if she touches the brothers," I say, joking. *Kinda.*

"You got it. I'm going to shower. If you want to come with, I can show you where the towels and hair products are. The academy keeps it stocked up for us," she says. "Don't worry, the showers have separate cubicles."

"Okay, I want to go and shower, but I can't keep what you said about the shower room being creepy out of my mind," I say, and she sighs.

"Okay, so a girl was killed in there by a dark descendant who managed to get into the academy," she explains, making a shiver drift over my skin when I feel a little fear. Not about the shower room, but about how a dark descendant could get in here.

"What? They can get in?" I whisper in horror, and she shakes her head.

"No, not usually anyway. Someone has to let them in. This girl was dating a dark tale and paid the price for it. She knew what she was risking, but the shower room freaks people out because that is where he killed her and escaped not long after," she says.

"Why would she date a dark tale?" I ask. "Was she crazy?"

"People do crazy things when they are in love with someone. Who knows why she risked her life other than she likely loved him," Tavvy answers. "I didn't know her, it was before I came here, so I'm clueless."

"Why would he kill her?" I muse. "If they were in love, it doesn't make sense that he would hurt her."

"They can't help themselves, usually. I've never seen or heard of a dark tale walking away from one of us before. The original goddesses made us enemies that cannot help but want to kill each other. It's almost as natural to us as breathing," she tries to explain to me. "I saw one once, just before he was killed, and the rumours of the draw to kill them are real. It floods your mind and makes you want to end their lives. Apparently, it is worse for them than it is for us."

"I hope I don't run into one of them then," I humourlessly chuckle and stand off the bed. "Though I'm not creeped out by the shower room. In most houses or places, someone has died in over the years. If I were scared of somewhere that people died, I wouldn't be able to go anywhere."

"I like you. I thought the same," Tavvy says and walks to the door, pausing before opening it. "Because I like you, I'm telling you what my mum and dad told me before I came here. One day, you will meet an enemy who was born to kill you. Make sure you're the one that comes out on top. Dark tales are out there, Madi, and you will meet one. So learn your powers that are your gift, and learn to fight back."

"My mum told me not to trust anyone," I quietly tell her.

"Seems our parents are pretty smart," she says sadly. "I think your mum was talking about the Tale brothers. A broken heart is likely the least of your problems if you're not careful with them."

"What do you mean?" I ask her as her hand goes to the handle of the door.

"Their parents are on the Masters' council and extremely powerful. The brothers disappear every other week for days at a time, and the school doesn't even ask where they go. Their previous fiancé turned up dead, and no one knows who did it. I saw Noah and Knox come back covered in dirt and blood one morning not long after she died…just be careful. They have dark secrets."

"I think the boys I remember as a kid are long gone," I admit. "I need to remember that when I see them. I need to remember things have changed."

"There is nothing boy about the Tale brothers. The sooner you learn that, the safer you will be."

Chapter 12

"Why do I need to wear stretchy clothes, Lane?" I ask Lane as I pull up the leggings that fit just a little bit tightly. I look over at the book I opened up and rested against my pillows after getting dressed in what he suggested for today. Lane just smirks as I pick up a black hoodie out of my wardrobe and put it over my tight clothes, hoping to cover up some of my skin on show. I glance in the mirror at the tight black leggings that go up to my mid waist and the light blue crop-top that hangs over one shoulder, short enough to show off my ribs. *Yeah, that didn't work.*

"What time is it?" Tavvy groans, before climbing down the steps of the bunkbed with messy hair sticking in all directions. She rubs her eyes and then pauses, staring at my outfit and then to Lane. "Oh god, it's Friday, isn't it?" she says with a long groan of annoyance.

"Considering yesterday was Thursday? Yep," I reply, and she grimaces at me like I just confirmed the world was ending.

"Wow, your second day at this school is going to suck. It's fight training class all day," she explains why she doesn't look happy and why Lane suggested stretchy clothes. I've never even punched someone before, how the hell am I going to survive fight class?

"Fight training?" I nervously question her, hoping she is going to tell me it's a big joke or something.

"Yep," she says, yawning and grabbing clothes out of the drawer as I go and sit on the bed. "Be prepared to get your ass whooped, but they have this healing cream that is amazing to mend you. So don't worry too much."

"There is no part about that sentence I don't worry about," I admit to her.

"Why are you up so early anyway? I thought Sleeping Beauty's descendant would like to sleep-in like yesterday," she asks me as she picks a brush up and starts sorting out her hair. "It took me an hour to wake you up."

"I get these bad dreams sometimes. I just couldn't get back to sleep, and I thought I might as well get up. Though I'm regretting it now," I say, covering up a yawn as she pulls her hair into a tight bun. I wonder if I should put my plaited hair up but decide I should just leave it.

"What do you dream of?" she asks, pulling off her pyjama dress and getting changed as I figure what exactly to tell her. The dreams don't even make much sense to me, and most of it, I try to make myself forget as soon as possible.

"Crows. Fire. People dying. The same dream I've had for months. It doesn't make sense and never changes," I admit to her, and she finishes pulling on leggings and a long vest shirt before replying to me.

"It might be a power of yours, you know. The dreams could mean something," she suggests.

"I don't think I even have any powers. Nothing weird has happened so far, and these dreams happened before I opened that book on my birthday," I explain to her. I guess the dreams could be trying to warn me of something, but I highly doubt crows, fire and dead people are clues of anything good.

"It takes fear, Madi, true fear to access your powers at the beginning. I got mine for the first time in fight class, so do most people," she tells me. "The teachers will let your opponent push you harder to see what you can do. As no one knows your powers yet, they will be expecting a show."

"Great, so I have to be close to peeing my pants to get my powers?" I sarcastically ask her.

"Yeah. I heard a kid actually did that once though," she says, making me more nervous, and she glances at my pale face as she pulls her trainers on. "We will skip breakfast because you might throw it up, now I think about it."

"Might?" I whisper.

"Actually, you will. We always run ten laps around the academy before we even start the practice fight. The teacher shoots the people at the back with streams of water from her hands if you fall behind or try to stop," she tells me. "Freezing cold ice water as well."

"Any chance I can just skip this class like yesterday's?" I ask, rubbing my hands together as I get more nervous.

"Nope. Even the Tale brothers don't skip this one. The academy is serious about fighting class above all else," she says, and I sigh, looking down at Lane.

"Any tips, Lane?" I ask him.

"Avoid pointy things," he replies. *Yeah, as if that isn't obvious.*

"I meant more along the lines of you explaining my family's powers and how I should use them, not general useless advice I already know," I say, and Lane grins at me.

"Your power is going to help you beat them all. I won't tell you though, it should be a surprise," he says and then fades away so there is only blue smoke left.

"That's not useful," Tavvy says, laughing. "At least my book told me I could use my dust to paralyse people. Oh, and make me and others fly."

"That's pretty cool. You could make me fly?" I curiously ask.

"Yeah, but only for a few moments. I'm not that good at it yet," she says, shrugging like it isn't a big deal when it is. "In a few years, I will get my wings, and it won't matter too much."

"Plenty of time to learn," I say, smiling at her just as there is a knock at the door. Tavvy walks to the door and pulls it open. She moves to the side a bit, so I can see where Oisin is standing outside with his arms crossed and a mysterious expression on his face as he spots me.

"Morning, ladies. Do you girls want a very good looking escort to class?" he asks.

"Yeah, we would love one. Do you know someone who has time to walk us to class?" I retort, and he laughs with Tavvy and me as I stand up. "But being more serious, that would be cool. We haven't had time to catch up much yet."

"I'm going to run and get some energy bars from the breakfast hall for us. Go ahead without me," Tavvy says, picking up her bag and winking at me before running out the room past Oisin. She tells me to stay away from the Tale brothers, and then in the next second, she leaves me alone with one of them. I close my book and put it in my bag before walking to Oisin who waits at the door for me to come out.

"Noah said you missed us," Oisin starts off, seeming like he couldn't wait to tell me that.

"Noah should learn when not to tell you guys everything," I reply. "He was never very good at keeping secrets."

"We were good at keeping secrets though, Sleepy. Just like that time two weeks before I left," he says as I shut the door, my hand pausing on the handle as a memory flashes through my mind.

"Oisin, stop it!" I squeal as he continues to tickle my ribs as I try to escape his grasp. I manage to get away only to trip on

the edge of my bed and fall backwards onto it. Oisin jumps onto the bed next to me, laughing as he grabs my arms and holds them tightly above my head with his one hand. My breathing quickens as I look up into his very unusual light silver eyes as they stare down at me, both of us losing the playfulness we had just a moment ago.

"You know, I've never seen anyone with eyes like yours or Knox's," I whisper, and his other hand gently cups my face. "I guess they are unique, just like you," he replies, his voice more gravelly than before, whereas mine sounds more high pitched than usual.

"I'm nothing special, Oisin," I say, laughing a little.

"Yeah, you are," he whispers back, leaning down and brushing his lips gently across mine. I freeze for a second, stunned that he would kiss me. Oisin never kisses me. I lean up and kiss him back, exploring his soft, yet firm lips as his hand releases my hands and slides under my head, pulling my head closer to him as the kiss deepens. The emotion and the way he kisses me makes me feel dizzy. I've always loved him and the others…just not like this. This is everything I didn't even know I wanted.

"Madi! Oisin! Dinner is ready!" my mum shouts up the stairs, and Oisin breaks away from me, crawls off the bed, and runs his hands through his hair as I stand up.

"Our secret?" I suggest, knowing his brothers and Quinton wouldn't take it well.

"Yeah, Sleepy. Our secret."

"*I*t's not like I had long to keep that secret. You disappeared on me not long after," I reply.

"You have to know we didn't want to do that. I thought Noah explained," he says. "I fought my parents all the way to the island, but we didn't have a choice."

"He did explain, but it doesn't stop it from hurting. You would understand if I walked away from all of you guys suddenly without a word," I reply, ignoring the way he looks at me like my words are cutting deep holes. "I thought there was more to us than that. When actually Quinton was the only one there in the end."

"Sleepy, you don't ever have to leave us all to make us know how much it hurts. Now you're here, you don't have to leave us, and more importantly, we don't have to leave you ever again," he says, grinning in that charming way that makes me want to instantly forgive him, and he knows it.

"We should get to class, Oisin," I reply, and he chuckles, stepping closer and wrapping an arm around my shoulders, pulling me to his side. I try not to breathe in how good he smells, but it is pretty impossible. He smells like peppermint.

"I thought you would be asking what my powers are. You were always so curious," he asks me after we have walked in silence for a few moments.

"I heard it was rude to ask," I reply, and he shakes his head as I stare up at him.

"Yeah, to ask someone random. We are family, we always have been. You know I'd tell you *anything* you asked me," he states, squeezing my shoulder.

"Alright then, what is your descendant power and is it as cool as being the sun or moon like Noah and Tobias?" I ask, and he rolls his eyes at me as we get to the main part of the corridor which makes me smile.

"*Merlin* was our descendant, and we come from one of the most powerful lines. Our parents were next in line to be Masters," he tells me. "Now we are. We both struggle controlling our unlimited powers, but we are getting better."

"Like *Merlin* the wizard? You guys are wizards?" I ask, and I must be getting used to hearing random things, because I'm not actually surprised.

"Not exactly. We have control over six elements. Though I'm better with fire, water and air, Knox has mastered earth, spirit and healing. We also each have our own particular strengths. I have enchantment powers, and Knox can pull anyone to another dimension he created," he tells me like it is nothing.

"We also can talk in our own dragon language. Though there aren't any dragons around anymore for that skill to be useful."

"Damn, that's pretty awesome!" I tell him, smiling up at him. "Remember when I told you I desperately wanted my letter from Hogwarts to turn up one day, and you told me I was a geek? Well, now who is the wizard, huh?" I tease him. All the guys hated watching *Harry Potter* on repeat with me, as they didn't like watching movies more than once, but I loved it. I guess I kind of got what I wanted, just a more fairy tale version of it with no powers to show. Okay, this isn't half as cool, but at least I know two wizards, it seems.

"You're still a geek, I see, just a very sexy one now. Not that you weren't always pretty," he says, twirling a strand of my hair around with his hand on my shoulder.

"Like Hermione?" I ask, ignoring the way my heart pounds at his compliment.

"That's your reply? No 'thanks for calling me sexy'? No red cheeks?" he asks, and I nervously laugh. "I guess that I'm going to have to work on my game."

"Sin, that kiss was just once, and I think we would be better as friends now. This is complicated enough, so no need to work on your non-existent game," I tell him, my thoughts straying to Quinton and how betrayed he would feel to see me flirting so soon after leaving him.

"I don't think we are better as friends. That kiss has haunted me for years, and I have no intention of letting you go again, Madi," he says, stopping me in the corridor and stepping in front of me. I look up at him as he stares at me, and I shake my head.

"Quinton and I—" I start off, and he presses a finger against my lips to stop me saying anymore.

"I know, and you must be feeling all kinds of fucked up since you left him. I know how that feels, Madi. I left someone I was in love with once as well." His honesty completely shocks me. I can only stare as he continues talking. "But life is short. Quinton was not meant for you, well, at least not just him. When you're ready to move on, I will be waiting. I've waited years to see you, a little more time isn't going to bother me."

"Oisin…" I whisper, watching as his serious expression turns playful once more.

"We have class, remember?" he says, winking at me and offering me a hand, making it clear he doesn't want to talk about this anymore. I slide my hand into his and let him silently lead me to class as

I think over and over about what he said. I don't know how to move on, I never really have. I always secretly hoped the brothers would come back, and I am still secretly hoping there is a way for Quinton and me to be together, even when I know it is likely hopeless.

Chapter 13

"Here," Sin offers me his bottle at the end of the ten laps as I lie on the floor next to where Tavvy has collapsed; both of us are worn out like most the class of twenty students sitting around us. Well, all of us except for Oisin, Noah, Knox and Tobias who are still standing. Tobias and Knox are jogging on the spot like lunatics. If I could lift my arms, I would find something to throw at them. I groan and look away, staring up at the white tiled ceiling.

"Thanks," I breathlessly say, accepting the bottle of water and drinking some big gulps before handing it back to him where he is hopping from foot to foot. "Seriously though, you guys are no fair." He laughs at my breathless grumble and runs off to his brothers who stayed at the front of all the runners the entire ten laps. I lie back down, calming my breathing down before looking over at Tavvy as she sits up and drinks some water.

"You did good, Madi. You only got hit with water like three times, right?" Tavvy asks me, and I shake my head.

"Four. I couldn't help but count the times the freezing cold water hit my backside. Though most of it got on my hoodie, and I took that off somewhere out there," I say as I sit up and glare at the sporty teacher who I know is evil from that run alone. She has dark brown hair up in a ponytail, a perfect skinny body, and she is wearing brown joggers with a white shirt. No part of her looks tired. I glance over to see Ella standing next to three guys, and she doesn't look that tired either. Though she has a little sweat on her skin, so she is at least a little bit normal like the rest of us.

"That was the easy part guys, I can't believe all you suckers are still tired! Maybe we should do extra running to build up your strength?" After nearly every person in the class protests instantly, the teacher laughs. "Alright. Alright. I was just messing with you. Everyone come here in a circle." I groan, making myself stand up even though most of my body protests against the idea. Tavvy links her arm with mine as we walk to the middle of the group and stop as the others join us. The brothers all watch me from the other side of the circle, and I look to my left as an arm brushes against mine, seeing a tall guy stood next to me, and he smiles. The guy is built like a tank, with a very small head, considering the size of his body. I think my head is the size of his arm. I look back to the teacher who is looking my way.

"Madilynn Dormiens, welcome to your first fight class. My name is Miss Aquana. As everyone already knows, I team you up into partners, and you combat the other until you win. Then when the bell goes, I team up the winners, and this goes on until there are two students left. Those two left battle each other, and the winner is the champion. The champion gets a prize of their choosing from a selection of pre-selected offers," she explains. "We offer everything from an hour on a laptop with Wi-Fi to a trip to a human town for shopping or food."

"How do you win?" I ask, curious.

"When your opponent is passed out or at least too badly injured to carry on. We have healers and creams to fix anything you can do. Though we prefer you perfect the art of knocking your class-mate out rather than hurting them too badly," she says. "It's no fun to have someone in the medic bay for weeks."

"I'm sure Miss Dormiens will struggle to knock out a fly, let alone beat one person in here. You don't need to worry, miss," Ella says, laughing through her words, and a few students around the room laugh. Even though she is being a cow, she has a point, if I'm being honest with myself. I can't fight. I'm not going to pretend I can. So, let's hope I have some secret powers, or this is going to be embarrassing. I glance at the brothers, who look tense as they watch me, but I smile at them anyway.

"Shut it, mermaid bitch," Tavvy snaps in annoyance. "Considering you've never won fight class, I don't know why you're talking."

"ENOUGH!" Miss Aquana shouts, making us all go into complete silence. "Right, Miss Dormiens will go against Roger. Why don't Octavia and Ella fight each other to work out some of that misused tension?" I glance at the guy at my left, wondering if he is Roger. By the grin he gives me, I wouldn't be surprised.

"Fine," Ella says in annoyance, whereas when I look at Tavvy, she seems pleased. Maybe Tavvy can beat her. I'm not sure my little fairy friend is all that innocent with the massive grin on her face at the moment. I think back to Roger, only noticing that the guy next to me is looking down at me with a smile.

"I'm Roger. Don't worry, I will go easy on you," he says, but I still gulp down a ball of fear in my throat as I nod at him, speechless. He only seems amused as he looks back at the teacher. I look to the brothers for comfort, but their angry expressions only make me more nervous.

"Everyone else, you can randomly choose your opponents today," she says, and everyone quickly walks off as Tavvy whispers to me while tugging my arm.

"Roger is Jack and the Beanstalk's descendant. He grows vines from his body, but he can feel them. Hurt the vines to win." I nod at her advice, watching her walk away before Miss Aquana waves a hand in front of her for us to join her. As Roger and I are walking over, I notice Knox and Oisin have teamed up nearby, and so have Noah and Tobias. Each one them is looking at me like I'm about to enter a death sentence.

"I will stay close and watch the fight as it is your first time," she explains to me. I glance around the massive gym room, which has large white rectangles drawn on the floor. There are three rows of them, and the students seem to stand at either end of the rectangles. We get an empty one in the middle of the room, and I move to stand at the opposite side of Roger.

"In three, two, one..." At the end of Miss Aquana's warning, she blows her whistle, and a ball of
water covers all of her body until she looks like she
is floating inside it, perfectly happy as she smiles at
me. I'm so distracted by Miss Aquana that I don't
see a massive green, leaf-covered vine heading
straight for my chest. It hits me hard, knocking the
air out of my chest, and I go flying straight across
the floor, my side taking most of the hit. I look up
just as vines slide tightly around my waist and lift
me into the air. I pull at the tight vines that start
spreading around my body, and then I hear
someone laughing. As I'm pulling, I look down to
see Roger holding his hands out, the vines coming
from them, and he is the one laughing.

"Stop, that's enough!" I hear someone shouting,
but I ignore everything as I keep trying to hurt the
vines with my nails and pull them off me. I try to do
anything, even leaning down to bite them, but I
can't reach. Nothing seems to work as they continue
to crawl up my body, and I glance around the room
to see the brothers being slammed with a wall of
water from Miss Aquana. As the vines get so tight
that they hurt, I grab at the ones that tighten
around my neck as I completely start to panic. I
scream as I try to pull them away, only hearing the
sound of Roger's laughing in the background as

black spots appear in my vision. Just as the black spots look like they are about to take me under, a cold feeling appears in my hands, spreading all over my body. Like an instinct, I move my hands away from the vines on my neck and stretch them out at my side. Suddenly, one word seems to be whispered into my mind. A word I struggle to say because the vines are so tight now.

"D-Dor-Dormiens!" I scream out, feeling a power like nothing I've ever felt before blasting out my hands, and the world seems to freeze for a moment. Then I'm suddenly falling to the floor at full speed. I hit the floor with a smack, the blast hurting my cheek, and I instantly place my hand against it, coughing from the impact. For a few moments, I can do nothing but breathe through the pain and try to concentrate on whatever the hell just happened. I pull the vines from my neck, and they easily fall away, the strength they had before is totally gone now. I suddenly wonder why it's so quiet. *Seriously, what the hell just happened?* I look down at my hands, seeing white glittering dust all over my hands, and the same dust is covering my body and the vines.

I stand up slowly, gaping at the room of students sleeping on the floor. Roger is at my feet, completely knocked out for the count, with white glittering dust all over his body. The brothers are passed out in a row not far away, and I can't see Tavvy through the mass amount of bodies. Only their moving chests and even snoring from a few tell me they are sleeping and that I didn't kill them.

When I hear clapping, I glance behind me to see a man I don't know, walking through all the students, stepping over a few like they aren't here. The man looks about my dad's age, but he has more grey in his blond hair and a few wrinkles that no doubt come from stress. The man has a full suit on, and I figure he must be another teacher. Remembering teachers, I look over at Miss Aquana passed out near me as well and assume I am going to be in trouble for knocking out the class. Somehow, I must have made that dust and knocked out the entire class, including the teacher. I don't think beating the teacher was part of the class. *Whoops.*

"You're simply amazing, Madi. I don't know any student that knocked out every single one of their classmates on their first day," he states, seeming proud as he finally gets to me. "I'm the supervisor here at Lost Time Academy, and I came to see if Miss Aquana needed any help. It seems she might, just not in the way I expected. I always assumed Sleeping Beauty's descendant would have premonition dreams and no outward powers. I am happy to be wrong." The supervisor stops rambling and laughs to himself.

I look around the sea of passed out students. "It was an accident...but do I win?" I ask. "I mean, everyone is technically passed out, and that was the goal. I am the last one standing." *It's worth a shot.*

"Well, there are no rules against using sleeping dust to make the class pass out. I guess you have won," he says with a smile, clapping his hands. "Oh, and by the way, my name is Mr. Newman. It is lovely to meet you, Miss Dormiens. I once knew your father when we were children, and I was so very sorry he didn't get powers. I know he will be extremely proud of you."

"I can't believe I could do that. I make sleeping dust, that is pretty cool," I admit to him, looking at my hands and wiping the dust off. Mr. Newman steps back, pulling a hanky out of his pocket and covering his mouth before speaking through it.

"I am going to get some help to wake everyone up. As you are clearly immune to your own powers, why don't you try waking some of them up while you wait?" he suggests.

"Okay, I can do that," I say, trying not to smile.

"Right then. I will be right back," he says and walks a little before looking back at me, his eyes seem calculating. "Congratulations on such useful and powerful defensive powers, Madilynn."

"Thanks," I reply quietly, but he is already walking away, and for some reason, I don't trust him. *I just don't know why.*

Chapter 14

"Wakey, wakey, Knox," I gently shake his shoulder as most of the class are waking up now after the teachers decided the best way was to wake Miss Aquana up and have her wash the class with water to get rid of the dust. Now, all of the class are soaking wet and looking at me like I'm their worst enemy as they try to stay awake. The class has been cancelled for the day, and most of them are walking back to their rooms to sleep it off.

"I wouldn't do that if I were you," Tobias goes to warn me as he sits up, and I frown at him. I go to move my hand away from Knox's shoulder, but then Knox suddenly grabs my arms, slamming me onto the floor and covering my body with his in a swift motion that makes my head spin. He grabs my arms, holding me tightly, and he doesn't even seem to be awake as I stare up at his narrowed, dazed eyes.

"Knox, wake the fuck up, man. It's Sleepy," Tobias says, moving closer.

"Knox, it's me," I lightly whisper to him, and he blinks his eyes, looking down at me in shock as he finally seems to wake up.

"Madi? What the fuck happened?" he asks me in a grumbly voice as he moves his hands near my head and leans his weight off me a little. "I was going to knock Roger the fuck out for taking it too far with you, and then everything is a haze."

"Err, well, I kind of put you and the rest of the class to sleep, accidently. Small bonus though, I won the prize!" I say, trying to not act nervous about or affected by all of Knox's hard, wet body pressed into mine. I can't do anything but stare up into his dark silver, almost swirling eyes that seem to burn with what I think is protectiveness mixed with an anger I don't understand.

"You put me to sleep?" he questions. "And the entire class while you were at it?"

"Yeah," I reply, and he quickly gets up off me, standing up and storming out of the room as I take a deep breath before sitting up.

"Knox never sleeps well, and waking up is

usually much worse for him. He once knocked
Oisin out, so don't take it personally," Tobias tells
me, offering me a hand to stand up as I finally look
away from Knox's tense back as he disappears from
sight. I slide my hand into Tobias's and let him lift
me up. Oisin and Noah are talking to the teacher
nearby, occasionally glancing at me as I search for
them.

"Knox never had that trouble sleeping before," I
reply, wondering what happened to him over the
years.

"I thought you would have guessed that things
have changed by now," he asks and suddenly frowns
at me, stepping closer. I freeze when he grabs my
chin lightly, turning my head to the side. "Your
cheek is bad, and it will bruise. Come with me."
After he finishes his assessment, he walks off like he
expects me to follow. I stare at him in confusion for
a moment, wondering why he seemed to care about
my face all of a sudden. He hasn't talked to me at
all since I got here, and I've barely seen him since
he sent Noah flying through the door on my first
day. I decide to follow him though, even if he is
confusing. Tobias walks to the other side of the
room where there are two doors. He holds the one
open for me, and I go to walk in just as someone
catches my arm gently, causing me to look back.

"I have the best and coolest roommate ever, that is all. See you back in our room," Tavvy tells me before letting go as I laugh and then spot Ella not far behind her as she walks past Tavvy to get to me.

"I have to admit, I am impressed," Ella tells me, yawning, "even if I don't like you, new girl."

"It kinda seems like you like me, Ella," I say, and she only laughs as I walk to Tobias and through the door he holds open. I enter a small room, with two cabinets and a medical bed pushed against the white walls.

"Sit on the bed," he demands.

"Yes, sir," I jokingly reply, and he shakes his head at me as I walk in and sit on the edge of the bed. My cheek does ache, now the buzz of the action in there has worn off. I no doubt will be left with bruises after all of this. I watch Tobias as he opens the cupboards and pulls out a green, small box before closing the doors and coming over to me. Tobias moves right in front of me, so my knees press against his thighs as he focuses on opening the tin. When he opens it, there is light blue shiny gel inside, and Tobias rubs some onto one of his fingers before reaching to spread it on my cheek no doubt, but I back away.

"I can put whatever that is on myself," I suggest. "I don't need your help or pity, Tobias. You've made it clear I mean nothing to you despite our past." My harsh words make him look up and meet my eyes, showing me some of the guilt I can see hidden in them.

"Just let me, Sleepy," he asks carefully, still keeping his eyes locked with mine. I find myself nodding in agreement, holding my breath as he gently rubs the gel into my sore cheek.

"Why didn't you come and see me?" I gently ask him, wanting to know. "Did you never think of me at all? I thought about you a lot, and even though you were so angry when I saw you first, I was happy to see you." My whole body lightly shakes from admitting any kind of feelings to a guy who doesn't seem to even care about me at all.

"You don't need to be nervous around me. I make everyone nervous," he replies, the movement of fingers on my cheek is so relaxing I could almost close my eyes if I didn't want to keep them on Tobias as I try to understand him.

"I'm not nervous around you, Tobias," I reply truthfully. "Why would you think that?"

"Everyone is," he replies. "You should be."

"I'm not everyone. I never was to you and the others. Or have things changed that much?" I ask, my heart beating in my chest at even saying it out loud. I almost feel like I don't know this Tobias at all. That I don't know the Tale brothers like I thought I did, because they have changed so much.

"You've changed, Madi. We've changed, but I thought after you saw how I was on your first day that you wouldn't want to know me," he admits. "I was angry at Noah over something, and you got in the way."

"Everyone gets angry, even me. I was angry at you once, remember? I threw my shoe at you, but you were still my friend," I reply, and he smirks at me for a second. "What happened with you two?" I ask quietly.

"Noah is a tool who thinks he knows everything. Simple as that," Tobias says, making me laugh, and even serious boy's lips turn up a little at the edges.

"I'm sure it is more than that," I say and flinch as Tobias's finger goes over my cheekbone where it is sorer. "Noah said you have been getting into things that aren't good for you."

"Noah still tells you everything, huh?"

"Not exactly. He didn't tell me what you are doing like I wanted," I reply, flinching again as he runs a finger over another sore point of my cheek. Tobias grumbles something and moves his hand away.

"I can help with the pain, soothe it for a little

bit, but you have to stay still. No talking," he warns me.

"Yes, sir," I reply, and he shakes his head but with a smile this time.

"Don't call me that, and stop being a cheeky little madam. Now hold still," he says and places his whole hand against my cheek. It hurts for a second before I feel a coolness spreading from Tobias's hand, making any pain fade away.

"The healing gel will kick in soon, but I can take away the pain for now," he tells me, and I automatically go to reply when he places a finger against my lip. "Shh, remember." I don't say anything or move at all as Tobias runs a finger across my bottom lip before moving his hand away suddenly. The door opens to the room, and Oisin walks in, staring at us both.

"I was going to see if you need any help, but clearly you are busy," he says and walks out before either of us can say a word.

"Oisin was always the jealous type. Everything from toys to food, he would never share. Yet the fact he didn't punch the shit out of me for being this close to you means he might have finally learned how to share for the right person. Funny that."

Chapter 15

"You can't wear that to the party tonight," Tavvy protests as I pull my hoodie over my leggings and shrug at her as she stares at me with her hands on her hips, a disgusted expression on her face.

"Why not?" I ask. This is what I would wear to parties back home. I don't think I even have a dress in my stuff I brought from home anyway. Tavvy tuts as I look at her green dress that compliments her blonde curly hair up in a messy bun and the light make-up she has put on. I've been too busy reading all the books the teachers have given me this week to even notice how Tavvy started getting ready the moment we came back from lunch. On Saturdays, thankfully, there are no classes, and we can do what we like. Tobias actually spoke to me at breakfast today with Oisin and Noah, but I haven't seen Knox at all, which is odd. I don't know if he is still mad at me for putting him to sleep. Everyone else seems to think I'm the coolest thing since sliced bread, and I don't know how to feel about that. I usually like to stay in the shadows rather than the spotlight, like at the moment, though I'm happy I won the prize, which turned out that the best one on offer was a phone call to my parents tomorrow.

"Madi, darling friend who is badass and beautiful. Please let me dress you for tonight. Like PLEASE," she asks in an overly dramatic way that makes me laugh. You can't help but love this girl.

"Alright, nothing too slutty though," I warn her, and she grins at me. I have the feeling she didn't hear a word of what I said past the part when I agreed to let her dress me.

"Put on those tight, black, high-waisted skinny jeans you have," Tavvy tells me as she goes through a box of clothes she had hidden under the bed.

"How do you know what clothes I have?" I ask her.

"I love fashion. I looked through your clothes on the first day to check there wasn't anything worse than that grease-stained hoodie," she says, not exactly apologising, but I don't really mind, if I'm honest with myself.

"My mum gave up years ago trying to help me understand fashion or what to wear. I'm happy in that hoodie," I tell her as I strip out of my clothes, leaving just my underwear on and pulling out the skinny jeans from the drawer under the wardrobe. I hate these ones, they are so tight, but they were Quinton's favourite, if I remember right. Not that I have anyone to impress, so...

"Your poor mum. Don't worry, I will not give up on you just yet," Tavvy says and then holds up a tiny little lacy top in the air for me to see. There is no back to the top, only the front which looks tight and like it will show off everything that my jeans don't cover up. I glare at her and shake my head as I take the top from her and pull it over my head, thinking this is better than a dress. Tavvy steps behind me as I look in the mirror, deciding that it doesn't actually look that bad. Tavvy undoes my hair from the plait and helps me shake it out, so it flows in curly waves all over my shoulders and down to my waist. I slide my flat shoes on, ignoring the little eye roll from Tavvy before she looks at the high heels of hers next to me, and I know she would prefer I try those on considering we are the same size. That is not happening. I would break my neck or worse with my luck.

"Damn, you look awesome! I'm so good!" Tavvy

says. "I would suggest a little make-up, but you know what, you have naturally long eyelashes and perfect skin anyway. So, no need."

"I don't know, it is a little revealing..." I drift off as someone knocks on the door, and I sigh as Tavvy opens the door. Ella is stood just outside in a black dress that is far more revealing than anything I could wear, and suddenly I feel a lot better. "Never mind."

"What are you doing here?" Tavvy asks, crossing her arms.

"We should walk together to the party," Ella suggests, and Tavvy laughs like Ella is crazy.

"You just want Madi to introduce you to the brothers," Tavvy says, and Ella grins, her dark red lipstick making the look seem more sinister than you would expect her smile to be.

"Whatever her reason is, let's go," I say, shaking my head at her and then suddenly remembering why I wanted to go to this party in the first place. I run back to my bed, using my body to hide the phone as I pull it out of the pillow and stuff it into my bra, the only place I can quickly think of.

"Seems new girl might be more interesting than I first thought," Ella muses, glancing at the little part of the phone that is sticking out. I quickly push it down, watching Ella to see what she will say next.

"Don't make me put you to sleep," I warn her. Not that I have a clue how to do that again.

"You have control over it already? I doubt it. But don't worry, I won't say a word," Ella says, walking down the corridor. Tavvy and I look at each other, knowing neither of us trusts her, but there really isn't much we can do about it right now. I shut the door behind us before walking down the corridor next to Tavvy.

We get to the end of the corridor and, instead of walking anywhere, Ella pulls open a random door which reveals a set of stairs. Tavvy follows Ella in first, and I go in behind her, pulling the door shut behind me before following them up the stairs. There are four flights of creaky, dark stairs before we get to the top where it opens up into a big empty attic room that looks like it stretches for ages. Ella doesn't step off the top step, she instead pulls a key out of her bra and holds it in the air. There is a flash of yellow light, and then Ella is gone.

"Creepy magic," Tavvy mutters and steps up to where Ella was just stood. "Hold my hand so we both go in together."

"Go in where?" I ask her slowly, still moving closer.

"The party," Tavvy says with a laugh, holding out a hand to me. I slide my hand into hers and step onto the top step next to her as Tavvy pulls out the white key we have from her bra and holds it in the air. There is a bright yellow flash again, and then we are no longer stood on a step looking at an empty room, we are on the same step looking into a massive party. There are flashing lights, loud beating music and dozens of students dancing, drinking and laughing. Ella stands tapping her foot near us, clearly bored of waiting for more than a moment. I let go of Tavvy's hand and step into the room, enjoying the warmth of the room and the feeling of just being someone normal. No one looks my way, too lost in themselves.

"Dammit, the brothers aren't here yet," Ella shouts over the music, and I roll my eyes at her, ignoring the stab of disappointment I feel that they're not here. I spot a table of drinks, dozens of bottles lining it, and I head straight for it. Now this is a party. I could use a drink, or a few, to loosen up and have a good night. Everything has been stressful since I got here, so heartbreaking, and I just want to do what normal teenagers do. So, drinking and then dancing until I forget who I am is the plan.

"Shots?" Tavvy loudly asks me, getting to the table at the same time as me and grinning. I pick up the tequila bottle off the table as Tavvy gets three little shot glasses from the back that don't look used. I look to my left as Ella comes to my side, her arms crossed in annoyance, and I smile at her. "Joining in, Ella?" Tavvy asks her in a daring tone.

"Go on then, fairy. Seems like I don't have anything better to do," Ella replies, and Tavvy just glares at her as she pours the shots before handing them out.

"One, two, three," I count and then down the shot with Tavvy and Ella at the same time. We do three more shots that burn my throat and make the room seem even warmer before I pick up a bottle of beer, and Tavvy helps me undo the lid as we all chuckle.

"Dance time!" I shout, loving the warm buzz and how Ella and Tavvy cheer with me. We all head to the dance floor a few moments later. I've never had girls as friends, but I like these girls for some reason. I laugh as I dance around, losing myself to the music and eventually losing Tavvy and Ella in the crowd as I dance away, avoiding other students. I drink my beer, hating the taste as I move my hips and slowly put my hands above my head, swaying to the music that seems to speak to me. I put the beer on a table somewhere before swaying my hips to a slower song in the middle of a big bunch of dancing people.

"Hey, party girl," a guy whispers into my ear before roughly pulling me back to him, his hands tightening around my waist before I can move away.

"Let go," I demand, trying to push him away from me, but it doesn't work, and he just holds me tighter. I try to wriggle out of his grip as he presses his head next to mine and kisses my ear. I start to feel my power in my fingertips just before the arms are ripped away from me, and I stumble a little as I try to stand up straight. I turn to see Knox holding a wiry young man in the air by the back of his jacket, but Knox's angry eyes are on me. There is silence as Knox lifts a beefy fist and punches the guy hard in the face. The jerk falls to the floor with a smack, and he doesn't get up. It should scare me, but the whole alpha thing just seems to do the opposite. *I like this side to Knox.* He is definitely the darkest one of the brothers now. The music is suddenly cut off as Knox walks to me in big strides and swiftly picks me up, throwing me over his shoulder before I can protest about it.

"Let me make this clear while you are all listening. Madilynn Dormiens belongs to the Tale brothers. Anyone touches her, and they deal with us." Knox's words seem to make everyone burst into whispers as Knox carries me out of the room.

"Put me down, Knox," I grumble, smacking my fists onto his back and trying to wriggle. His arm is like a vice grip on my thighs though, and I don't move anywhere.

"Nope. You are drunk, and I don't trust you not to fall over or throw up," he says, walking down the stairs which actually does make me feel sick with every movement as my head bounces against his back. We get out to the corridor and instead of going towards my room, he turns and walks to the other stairs in the corridor, banging my head more against his back as we go up it.

"My room is back there," I tell him, my fuzzy head making everything a bit uncertain. Do I have a room upstairs? Who knows?

"I know. I said I don't trust you not to be sick, so I am watching you for the night in our room," he informs me.

"Our room? Won't your roommate mind you are having a girl over for a sleepover?" I say and then giggle to myself. "Well, not *girl*-girl over for the night. We don't do that. Do we?"

"Dear god, stop talking, Sleepy. My brothers and I share a room like we always have done," he tells me, and I nod my head, even though I'm slightly aware he can't see me do it.

"Where are the others?" I ask him. "In the room?"

"No. They are out for the night doing some-thing important. We take turns making sure you are okay, but I didn't expect you to be the party animal like I found tonight," he says, his words gruff. "Also, where the hell did you learn to dance like that!?"

"You should lighten up, Knox, and join the party! We could have danced together!" I say, and he chuckles.

"You are drunk as hell, Sleepy," he says, and I hear him opening a door and walking us into a room. Knox gently places me on the floor, and I grin at the four different versions of him I can just see before the world blacks out.

Chapter 16

I groan as I wake up, rolling into the musky, chocolate-smelling pillow and stretching my legs out, feeling the silky sheets wrapped around me. It's not until I blink my eyes open, hating the bright light from a window that is shining into my eyes, that I realise I am not in my bed. I sit up sharply to see where I am, immediately holding a hand to my head to stop it from pounding so loudly from the movement. A wave of dizziness overtakes me as I try to make my mouth less dry. I clear my throat a few times until the dizziness stops and I feel sure I'm not going to throw up. I haven't felt this shitty in a long time. What the hell happened last night? I'm sure I didn't drink that much, though I only really remember the shots with the girls…then everything else is a blur. I likely don't want to remember, considering I'm in someone else's bed. Another wave of dizziness hits me as I try to move again, and I squeeze my eyes shut.

"Oh god, I'm dying," I groan and hear a set of very familiar chuckles. I blink one eye open to see Noah and Knox in the room with me. Knox is lying on the floor with a pillow and blanket, whereas Noah is in the bed opposite me in the room. Both of them have messy sleep hair, and they are shirtless. *Why is Knox on the floor?* This must be their room. There are two sets of bunkbeds, two wardrobes, a chest of drawers, and their room is massive. There is even another door open in the room, and it leads to a bathroom.

"No, you are hungover. Sin went to get you something to help," Noah tells me, sitting up, and the blanket seems to slowly fall down, revealing his naked chest. I gape at the tight muscles on show, the *z* tattoo on his ribs, and all the way back up to his very amused face. I shake my head, only regretting doing so straightaway as I put my head into my hands.

"What happened last night?" I ask quietly. "And when the hell did you get a tattoo?"

"Drunk Madi can dance way too fucking hot. I'm never letting her go to a party alone again,"

Knox fills me in, though he speaks like I'm not actually here, and it all comes rushing back to me like a smack to the face. I peep through my hands to see Knox has sat up, and he smiles at me in a playful way.

"I just wanted some fun," I groan, wanting to hide my face as it burns red at Knox's statement.

"I get that. Next time, invite us," Noah suggests. "We wouldn't have said yes to our job if—" Noah stops mid-sentence as a pillow goes flying at him from above my bed. What the hell kinda jobs are teenagers doing on a Saturday night? I go to ask not only where the pillow came from but what work they are doing, as someone shouts.

"Shut it, will you, before I make you keep your mouth shut. It's like six in the morning on a fucking Sunday," Tobias's grumbly voice comes from above me, and then I hear him rolling over as I chuckle low with Knox and Noah.

"I see he still isn't a morning person," I whisper as Noah puts his pillow behind him, resting back on it and making no move to pull the blanket up, so I'm stuck staring at his naked chest.

"You aren't usually either," Knox states, and he has a point. "I thought I'd have to wake you up at some point."

"Nope, I'm up and sort of alive. I'm going to

use your bathroom," I state, not really waiting for their replies as I get up. I slide out of bed, looking down at the red shirt someone has put on over my clothes from last night, and when I stand up, the shirt goes to my knees. "Which is unfair that you guys have your own bathroom, and we girls don't get that."

"Boys rule, and you know it," Noah teases.

"I think you'll find 'girls rule and boys drool' was the song," I reply just before stepping into the bathroom and hearing his reply.

"The song was right about boys drooling over hot girls like you, Madi." I roll my eyes at his flirting and shut the door. After using the toilet, I wash my face with some water and smooth down my messy hair. I rub my teeth with some of their toothpaste, and when I straighten my top under one of the guys' shirts, I feel the phone in my bra still. *I can't believe I forgot last night.* I suddenly think back to the real reason I went to the party, one I seem to have completely forgotten last night. *I need to call Quinton.*

"I have to go. Thanks for, well, being there for me last night," I say as I open the bathroom door.

"Where are you off to?" Noah asks, sitting up at my words, and I look around for my shoes, not seeing them straightaway.

"I'm going to the roof after getting my book

and asking Lane to tell me where to go," I explain, and Noah looks at Knox before back to me.

"Why the roof?" he asks, and he looks worried. Part of me doesn't want to admit that I'm going to call Quinton.

"Why the million questions suddenly?" I counter in avoidance, and he flashes me an annoyed glance as I look away from him to Knox. "Thank you for looking after me last night. Whatever I drank was stronger than I thought."

"There was magic in the drinks, making them three times stronger than usual," Knox replies. "And it was nothing. I'm always here, that hasn't changed."

"Right, just everything else has changed. Well, thank you anyway," I reply, feeling a bit awkward as I look around the room for my shoes again and finally spot them by the door. I go to them, feeling all the guys' eyes on me the whole time. I start to say goodbye when the door opens, and Oisin walks in, holding a carry out mug with something sweet-smelling in it.

"Morning, Sleepy. Here you go," Oisin says, looking proud to hand me whatever the drink is. I accept it and grab the door he is about to close, holding it open.

"Thank you for this, and I will see you later," I

tell him, going to step out, but he places a hand on the door, his arm blocking me from leaving. I meet his playful silver eyes that have that seductive swirling way about them like his brother's do. I never knew silver eyes could be attractive, but damn, his are.

"Where are you off to so quickly?" he asks me. I groan, knowing I'm not going to escape as easily as I had hoped.

"I have things to do, Sin. Out of the way," I say, using my hand to attempt to push his arm out of the way, but it is like an arm of steel or something. I drop my hand and just glare at him until he drops his arm.

"Not without me, you don't. I wanted to hang out with you today," he says.

"Oisin knows his way to the roof, so that's a good idea for him to go with you," Knox interrupts, and Sin gives me a curious look.

"Why the roof?" Sin asks me.

"I want to see the sun rise," I lie to him, and I know not one of them believes me in here because of the way they are all smirking as I look between them. The only one that isn't listening in is Tobias as I can hear his light snoring.

"Alright. I'm down to join you. Let's go," Sin says, and I was hoping he would change his mind. I don't know how well the guys are going to take me talking to Quinton. Either way, my heart beats a little faster at the idea that I will be able to speak to him. It feels like it has been years when it has only been days since I got here. I open the lid to the drink Sin gave me, as he shuts the door behind us, and take a long sip. The drink is warm with a minty flavour that somehow makes me feel so much better with only a few sips.

"What is this stuff?" I ask as he gets to my side and wraps an arm around my shoulders. The academy is pretty cold this early, and I'm happy to snuggle into his side.

"We like to have parties in our room, mainly the guys only though, so we have this stuff to fight the hangover off. It's a mix of the healing gel and herbal tea. Pretty good shit, right?" he replies, and I grin around my cup lid.

"You're right, it's pretty good shit. Thanks," I tell him, and he kisses the side of my head.

"Anything for you, my sleepy Madi."

Chapter 17

"It's a pretty view," Sin comments once he helps me up the final steps of the ladder to the roof. The roof is mainly flat, with tiny walls around the perimeter and several chimney tops dotted around the stone roof. I glance around at the pink, orange and spots of red sky as the sun rises over the forest that surrounds the academy. *It is stunning.* "Now tell me why we are *really* up here, Sleepy." I glance over at Sin, seeing his arms crossed tightly against his chest, the tight expression he has on his face makes me think he already knows. I pull the phone out of my bra, and he sighs, shaking his head.

"Knew it," he says. "You want to call Quinton."

"Yes," I reply, avoiding his gaze. I don't know why I feel guilty about it, but some part of me does.

Maybe it was just the way Sin asked. Maybe it was something more.

"Go on then. Call him," he suggests, even when he doesn't seem happy about it. I nod and walk over to the middle of the roof, sitting down with my back resting against the brick chimney. Sin comes and sits next to me as I turn the phone on, reading the dozens of messages from Quinton first. Each one breaks my heart, each one is worse than the last until the final message which only confuses me:

Sleepy, just call me when you can. Or I will come for you. Don't trust anyone and remember I love you.

"What do you think he means by that? He sent it on the day I left, and there hasn't been a message since," I ask Sin, knowing he read the message with me.

"Neither of us will know until you call him," he replies, nudging my shoulder. "Just remember you can't tell Quin anything about this world. I know it will be hard, because there were so many times I just wanted to pick up a phone and call you, tell you everything. But I wouldn't risk someone's life that I care about more than my own."

"You can be super sweet at times, Sin," I say, sadly smiling as my heart beats loudly.

"Don't go telling that to anyone else. It might ruin my reputation," he says, and then his lips tighten as he looks at the phone in my hand. "Call him." I don't say anything else to Sin as I press call on my phone and put it to my ear as it rings. On the fourth ring dial, Quin picks the phone up.

"I didn't expect to ever hear from you again," he says, his voice gruff like I just woke him up, but I can hear a longing in his voice that matches how much I wanted to hear his voice too.

"I'm sorry. I wish I could explain," I start off, but then I just pause because I can't explain, and I don't even know what I want to say.

"I know you can't," he tells me. "I know everything."

"I highly doubt that Quin," I reply, because he couldn't know everything. That wouldn't make any sense.

"Don't call me again, Madi. Never. Do you understand me?" he asks, not sounding one bit like my Quinton. My heart breaks at his cold words with their tone of finality.

"I didn't leave to hurt you. Don't hurt me like

this. I only wanted to speak to you for a moment. Check that you are okay," I explain to him, my voice is more desperate than I expected to sound.

"I'm bad for you. For everyone. I mean it, Madi, don't call me again…because I can't stop myself from answering. Be safe. Keep the Tale brothers close, and always remember I love you," he says, and then the phone beeps, signalling he hung up. I let the phone drop from my hand in my confusion and shock.

"He knows, Sin. I think he knows everything, but how?" I ask Oisin, who looks as shocked as I do, as he must have heard that conversation just like me.

"I don't know, that was strange. How could Quin know we are with you?" Sin asks, picking up the phone and turning the phone off before handing it back to me.

"I miss him," I admit.

"Do you love him that much? Enough to let him go?" Sin asks me, and I rest my head on his shoulder, looking at the sun rising high in the sky. I don't have an answer.

"Maybe."

"Is there room for more than one person in your heart, Madi? Because you are not alone. We will figure it all out if you will let us help you," Sin assures me. I tilt my head up, seeing that he is looking down at me. I don't know why I do it, but I move closer and brush my lips across his. Sin makes this content noise at the back of his throat as he slides a hand into my hair and kisses me back. I don't know how long we are on the roof, but I do know one thing. I'm not alone at Lost Time Academy, even if my heart feels lost. Time will tell what happens, but as I kiss Sin, I know it can't be that bad, no matter what happens. *After all, I have the Tale brothers.*

Chapter 18

"*T*his way, Miss Dormiens," Miss Ona instructs after I knocked on her office door, and she came out a few moments later. I was told to come here to claim my prize after dinner, before bed. It is a call to my parents which I desperately need after that talk with Quinton yesterday and the kiss with Sin. Thankfully, Sin hasn't bought it up this morning, and I'm not sure I really want him to. Maybe we both can just understand that we equally needed comfort. I'm not emotionally ready to be in any kind of relationship, I know that. I still need to find my feet here in my new life, and the Tale brothers are keeping a million secrets from me that I want to know. I think they are in trouble, but I don't know much of the new world I've found myself in to ask the right questions to get the answers I want. I spent all night going over and over whether I should just call Quinton back and demand he tell me what I want to know. Like how the hell he knows I'm with the Tale brothers. It doesn't make sense. Humans aren't meant to know anything about us, and the fact Quin might makes me scared for him. Even if we can't be together, I want—no need—to know Quin has a good, safe life.

"Do you know the Tale brothers' parents, Miss Ona?" I ask her as she leads me down the corridor, and I eye her carefully. I'm extremely curious what these teachers have for powers and what fairy tale they are from. Miss Ona is the nicer one of the sisters, but I doubt she would tell me if I just flat out asked her. She almost pauses in her step at my question but continues on down the corridor and around the stairs. I have fleeting memories of the brothers' parents, because they were never around or at least not enough to be considered real parents. The brothers had a nanny who did everything for them, and their parents were always travelling. They would come back for the brothers' birthdays and sit silently in the room as they had their parties and opened their presents. I asked my mom about them once, and she simply told me some people are not meant to be parents. That they don't have the maternal side to them that parenting needs. Though now I know they are Tale descendants, I'm wondering if there is a lot more to the story. Maybe I judged them too quickly.

"The brothers' parents are on the Masters' council, along with two other powerful families. Ella is another descendant with a parent on the Masters' council. I do not know them, not many do, but I am aware that they have a difficult job keeping us safe. We are at war, and in this academy lies the most precious treasure at stake in the war," she tells me, glancing back at my face for a second.

"Which is?" I ask.

"The young descendants. Young minds with incredible powers and all that is left to breed the next generation of their enemies. The dark tales' leader is cruel, heartless and childless. He has made it clear he wants the academy and the students many times. We must keep you safe, do you under-stand?" she asks me, stopping to make sure she gets my answer.

"Yes," is all I can find myself saying. Why would he want us though? Surely he wants us dead, to kill off the competition more. We walk in silence until we get to the end of the corridor, where it is dustier than the usual places of the academy.

"In here is a phone, and your parents' number is

written down on paper next to it," she instructs, pointing a hand towards the door, and she lowers her hand, turning her head to the side as she looks at me. I'm glad the number is written down, because who knows phone numbers now? "You might be the most powerful student we have ever had, and your line is very much hidden in clouds, so we are unsure how strong you will be. It is important you focus on training and conditioning yourself for war, because it is close. Love and relationships must take a back seat in what is to come. Love cannot protect you from death at the hands of the dark tales, Miss Dormiens."

With those solemn words, she walks away down the corridor, leaving me holding the straps to my bag as I watch her go. I shake my head, pushing her words to the back of my mind to get them out of the way before going to talk to my parents. I know Miss Ona is warning me to stay away from the brothers, to not let love cloud my training and take over. Only, I think the Tale brothers might actually be able to help me. I need knowledge on how to fight on my own, something my parents never taught me growing up. I make a mental note to ask one of them to teach me, as I open the door and walk into the small classroom. The room is empty now, covered in dust and cobwebs except for the one table with a phone and a piece of paper on it, in the middle of the cleared out room. I let the door swing closed behind me as I go to the chair, sitting down and picking up the paper. The phone is old school with big clumpy numbers and an actual dial tone. After I finish putting the numbers in, the phone starts ringing, and I sit back in my seat, praying that someone answers. After a few rings, the phone is picked up.

"Hello, who is it?" my mum says in the same way she always answers the phone. It's not a nice, welcoming answer, but it's because mum says her real friends text her, and only scammers call her. It always made me smile to hear her telling off a scam caller as she made herself a cup of tea. I can't help but smile wide enough that my mouth hurts at hearing her voice.

"It's me, mum," I tell her, and she squeals down the phone before shouting for my dad.

"I'm so happy to hear from you. Are you allowed phone calls there then?" she asks, sounding surprised, and the tone changes, making me aware she has me on speaker now.

"No, I had to win fight class to get one phone call to you guys," I say, and I hear my mum's joyful shout and my dad's loud, proud laugh.

"You won fight class? But how?" she sputters after calming down. "Are you hurt?"

"I'm fine. My power is to create sleep dust, and I knocked out the entire room, including my teacher. I am going to learn to control it, but it's a good start," I explain to them. It's weird to know I have this power now, and I can actually protect myself, even though I've not exactly mastered controlling it yet.

"I am so proud of you," my dad says in the background, as I'm clearly on speaker phone. "My girl, knocking out a whole class in her first week." I can't help but laugh at his proud and happy voice. It's not something every dad is happy about, but we aren't normal. Honestly, we never were, and I love that.

"Hey dad," I say.

"Hey darling. We miss you, and we are so proud you are settling in well," he replies to me, and I take a nervous deep breath before asking a question I need to know.

"D-did Quinton come asking for me? Is he okay?" I ask after a moment, knowing I need the answer no matter how nervous I am to ask. Quin still makes my heart pound, my mouth feel dry, and everything so much more. The Tale brothers do it to me as well, they always have done. When we were all together, it was perfect.

"The boy didn't come here, and being your dad, I went to his house to check he was alright. He moved out, both him and his mother," he tells me, making me more nervous than ever before. What the hell is going on with Quin? He wouldn't move out, he couldn't. They lived in a trailer on some rent free land, and it was the best they could afford. His mum wouldn't move them out, because she lived rent free, and the rent money would go to buying fags and booze. Quin wouldn't give up his job either, or his school, because that was his entire future.

"What?" I finally whisper when my thoughts finally let me breathe. This doesn't make me feel any better about any of this.

"Madi are the Tale boys there? Did they remember you?" mum asks. Ah, they knew the brothers where here and where they went when they left. Of course they did. My parents watched me cry for weeks when they disappeared, and they couldn't tell me the truth. I want to be mad at them for that, but I get it. Telling me the truth then was illegal to the tales descendants, and they had to let me suffer. Quin was there though, and now he is going through what I did but much worse. We were each other's first time, first date, and well, most things except for first kiss…and now he is alone. I feel so guilty, even though it isn't my fault. I can't go back to him.

"They aren't boys anymore, mum, and yeah, they did. We are friends again, just like no time passed at all," I tell her, and I can hear her smile through the phone, even without seeing it. Dad grumbles about something, but I just miss it. The phone starts loudly beeping, and I quickly realise I don't have long left.

"You have to go, don't you, darling?" dad asks me, sounding sad. I'm not used to hearing my dad sound anything but cheeky and happy.

"Yeah, seems so. I miss you guys. I really do. How long do I have to stay here again?" I ask, as I've forgotten.

"Oh Madi, we miss you more than anything in the world, and we are proud of you. It can't be that bad there," mum replies, and I sigh.

"It's not that bad here, I just miss home," I reply and leave out Quinton's name in that. I can't help but worry about him more now than I was before, and there is nothing I can do about it. Quinton asked me not to call him again, and I really should respect his decision because it is his to make. Maybe he just moved away for a new start and his mum buggered off. At least I want to try and convince myself that is true, even if I don't believe it.

"We love you," mum replies, and then the dial tone rings, ending the call. I drop the phone back into the holder, staring at it like it's going to ring and give me the closure I need. *It can't.* I look out the window in the room, seeing the dark sky, the millions of stars littering it, before I yawn. I could really do with a night of long, deep sleep. Hopefully, my dreams will not be creepy and give me more closure than being awake does. I climb out the seat, walk to the door and pull it open only to find Knox leaning against the wall on the other side of the corridor.

"Hey, you alright?" I ask, because hell, he doesn't look it. Knox seems, well, tired. I yawn after he does because yawns are super contagious. I'm sure of it.

"I need a favour. One only you can help me with," Knox tells me, pushing up off the wall. The dim light shines against his face more now, and his eyes lock with mine.

I don't even think twice before answering. I'd do anything to help the brothers. "Anything."

Chapter 19

*K*nox offers me a hand rather than telling me what the favour is, and even though it's been years since Knox and I held hands, my hand slides into his like no time has passed. That's the thing I'm noticing with the brothers, it feels natural and safe like it always has. We aren't kids anymore, and yes, things about us all have seriously changed, but in so many ways, it hasn't at all. Knox stares down at me for just a moment, letting me see the dark shadows under his eyes which make the dark silver colour of them that much darker. It doesn't suit his blond hair, which is darker than his brother's now and longer, falling across his forehead. Knox looks stressed and tired, but even like this, there is something so attractive about him. That is one thing that changed between us all: the tension. It was there a little bit before, but now it's always there. In a matter of seconds, he turns away and gently tugs on my hand to lead me back down the corridor.

"How was your chat with your parents?" he asks me, making me fully aware that the Tale brothers are seriously keeping an eye on my butt. I knew they were taking turns watching me, because there is nowhere I can go without a Tale brother nearby, and they told me as much. I want to tell them to chill, but I'm clueless about this world, and every-thing I'm learning isn't making me trust it any more.

"Good. It helped, but I still miss them," I admit to him, keeping my voice low as I don't want anyone else hearing that. Though the corridor is quiet, and I can hear people talking nearby and in the classrooms we pass.

"You were always close to your parents, it's normal to feel that way," he states, trying to make me feel better.

"Do you miss yours?" I ask, almost predicting the answer straightaway he gives me.

"No. We get letters from them weekly, so it is hard to miss them when they are still so involved in controlling our lives," he coldly replies, though that tone is and always has been there when he speaks of his parents. They never talked much of them growing up, and I don't blame them. It was my mum or their nanny who gave them hugs and loved them. Money and a big house don't make a happy home.

"They are on the Masters' council...and you will be one day, I presume?" I ask, starting to understand how this all works a little bit. For the last week, I've been staying up late at night to read as much as I can to understand the world I'm now a part of. It's pretty simple from what I have figured out. The Masters rule, their children take over, and then they rule. It's been that way for a long time, and all the laws are from the Masters.

"One day, and maybe we might stand a chance at keeping us all alive. Right now, as it stands, they are going to get us all killed," he remarks, sounding angry and cryptic at the same time.

"Why?" I whisper as we pass a group of students and start climbing the stairs. Knox tugs me closer at the top of the stairs, keeping his voice low. My body presses against his, and my hand somehow finds its way to rest on his flat stomach, his thin jumper doing little to hide how firm he feels. Knox doesn't seem to notice the effect he has on me, he just keeps talking as I try to hide my feelings.

"The dark tales have a new leader who isn't attacking us anymore, and he has pulled his army back. My parents and the others believe that they have given up, and they are hoping for peace. Yet, it isn't logical. I believe the leader is gathering his army and making a plan. God help us all if he is, because my parents and the whole tales community isn't ready for an attack," he whispers to me. "We are weaker than ever, too lost in the old ways."

"If that doesn't frighten you, then I don't know what else would," I say, because that scares me and makes me want to run away, hide in the human world with my family, and pretend I'm nothing but human. I've not even met a dark tale yet, but they sound terrifying.

"You don't need to be frightened, Sleepy. I would die before letting a dark tale anywhere near you," he fiercely tells me. We both pause at the end of the staircase to the guys' room level, staring at each other as I believe every single one of his words. In this moment, I forget how my heart still hurts for Quin, how I'm confused about my feelings for Knox's brothers and everything other than how much I want to know what it is like to kiss Knox. Not the brief first kiss we had at eleven, no, I want to know what it would be like to really be with Knox. The moment is broken when a guy clears his throat from behind us, and we quickly move out of the way as I instantly feel guilty. Damn, this is all confusing. Knox tugs my hand with a cautious smile before leading me up the stairs and to his room. Knox pushes the door open with one hand, letting go of my hand so he can turn a lamp on which is near the door. The room is empty, though a little messy, but then four guys live in here, so that could be expected. It doesn't smell bad; that's a small bonus.

"What is the favour then, Knox?" I ask him as I shut the door, and he clears his throat, looking awkward as he turns to answer me.

"I need you to put me to sleep. With your powers," he requests, and I really didn't expect that. He does look tired, but putting him to sleep is dangerous for me. I have no control. I could accidently put the whole school to sleep.

"Why?" I ask.

"Let's just say I have bad dreams, and I can't sleep well since..." he drifts off, clearly not wanting to tell me what haunts him. "I haven't slept more than an hour in a long time. I'm exhausted, getting paranoid, and I can't take this much longer. Though when you used your powers, I finally slept well and peacefully. I can't forget it. Please, Sleepy. I need you."

"Knox, maybe talking about what happened will help too," I say, wanting to help him more than just put him asleep. There is also the problem that I have zero idea how to use my powers. What I did in the fight class was pure instinct.

"I c-can't," Knox tells me, and I try not to feel hurt that he is keeping something from me, but when I look into his eyes, I know it's something that is bad. So bad that he is trying to protect me from it.

"Okay, but I eventually want the truth. The only problem left is that I don't know how to control my powers," I say, knowing this all could go wrong, but there is no way I will walk away from Knox when he needs my help. Maybe if he could sleep for a while, he might tell me what is haunting him.

"I will guide you through it," Knox says with a relieved smile. I might not know what is going on with my Tale brothers, but I am damn sure going to find out. Knox goes and lies down on his bed, placing his hands behind his head as I follow him over. I sit on the edge of the bed, my back pressed against the side of his chest as he looks up at me.

"Place your hand over my face, hovering it almost," he instructs me as he closes his eyes. I do as he instructs, waiting for more instructions, feeling his hot breath blowing against my palm. It's almost sexy and not helping my concentration at all.

"Done," I whisper.

"Close your eyes, Sleepy," Knox tells me, and I close my eyes, sighing when I don't feel anything but stupid. I go to tell Knox this when he starts talking himself.

"Our power is found deep within our souls, next to the part of us that feels great emotions like love, hate, loss and many others. When I call my powers, I find that part of me that is always there and always has been. It's right there, Sleepy. You only have to believe and trust in yourself to find it." I run Knox's words over in my mind, thinking of so many people I care for. So many people that I know I love in a way that isn't easy to explain, even to myself. There is something else there though, just like Knox explained. I focus on the warm feeling in my chest, and just like a button is clicked, everything changes. The power feeds through my body like a cold wave of water, making sure I'm aware and awake even though my power is sleep. I hear Knox gently snoring only a second later and I open my eyes, seeing white sparkling dust softly falling from my hand over his face.

"Madi, you are incredible," I hear Noah say as I stop my power and turn to see he came into the room at some point. Noah looks at me in wonder with a proud smile as I wipe my hand of the left-over dust and stand up. I try not to blush at Noah's compliment, but ah crap, my cheeks burn anyway.

"Will you walk me back to my room, Noah? Knox needs some sleep," I ask, and Noah only grins at me as he offers me a hand to hold.

"I'd happily walk you back, Madi," he replies. I link my hand with him, looking back once at Knox who is peacefully sleeping before we quietly leave their bedroom.

"How long has Knox been struggling to sleep, Noah?" I ask him, waving at two girls who pass us who are Ella's friends. I don't know their names as I'm pretty forgetful, but they are nice. The nice girls are called... Crap, who knows?

"About seven months, since..." Noah clears his throat. Dammit, they are all keeping something big from me, and I can't even guess what it is because I haven't been here. I remember Tavvy saying something about their fiancé dying...but I know the Tale brothers wouldn't have had anything to do with that. They aren't killers, at least I don't think. Not *that* much could have changed in these last few years.

"Don't you trust me? I'm not going to judge you guys about whatever it is that Knox isn't sleeping over, Tobias is messed up from, Sin seems to be pretending never happened, and you...well sometimes you seem sad. I just want to know what the hell happened," I ask him, wrapping my hand around his arm to make him look at me.

"We all agreed not to speak of it. To anyone," he tells me, quickly looking away.

"And I'm just *anyone* to you guys?" I ask, feeling hurt from that response. They are far more than anyone to me, but perhaps it's not the same for them.

"It's complicated, Sleepy. I will talk to them about telling you, because you are right, you are not *anyone*," Noah promises, but it doesn't stop me from feeling hurt over this all. I nod once at him, telling him I'm thankful, before we walk silently until we get to my room. I know being upset isn't going to help them or me. It's pointless, and I just have to hope they will open up to me.

"Noah, will you train me to fight? Magic sleep dust is a cool power, but useless unless I can protect myself," I ask him, because I briefly saw Noah and Tobias fighting, and he looked incredible.

"Yeah, I can do that. How about every Sunday, we spend the day training?" he asks, squeezing my hand once before letting it go.

"Perfect. Thank you," I say, though it still feels awkward with this unspoken thing.

"I'll see you in class tomorrow, Sleepy," Noah says and leans forward, pressing a brief kiss on my cheek. He leaves me speechless as he walks off down the corridor, and I can only watch him go.

Chapter 20

"*I*'m pretty sure Miss A is still pissed about the last fight class," I breathlessly groan, leaning on Knox's shoulder as Tavvy laughs. We are all drenched in water, thanks to Miss A insisting we run laps around the gym today quicker than last week. Of course, the guys are not out of breath at all, unlike Tavvy and me. If anything, they look happy and ready to take on the world. I just want to put my butt into bed and stay there for the rest of the day. If I could have Netflix and chocolate, then I'd be a happy girl. Knox smiles down at me, looking so much more relaxed and, well, healthy since I've been putting him to sleep with my dust every night this week. Tobias avoids my eye contact when I look at him, but considering he has avoided me all week, I'm not overly shocked. Noah and Sin are talking together a good distance away, laughing at something, but it makes me smile to see them so relaxed.

"Just don't knock her out this time, babe," Knox suggests, and I grin at him as Tavvy laughs, finally getting her breath back with me.

"Good luck today, new girl. I don't fancy sleeping this class today, so learn some control," Ella sarcastically comments as she passes by me. *Bitch.* Tavvy sneers at her as she walks past, and Miss A chooses that moment to blow her whistle and call the class together. My hands shake as we circle around her, and Knox, like he can sense how nervous I am, slides his hand into mine.

"You got this, Sleepy, and I'm always close by. No one will hurt you," he tells me, trying to make me less nervous, but it doesn't work as Roger pushes through the crowd and comes to my other side.

"Hey, we didn't get to talk after you knocked me out, but I was impressed," he says, offering me a hand to shake. I shake his hand, actually pretty impressed he is saying anything to me about that. Usually guys don't like to be beaten by a girl and won't talk about it, let alone come and shake my hand. I want to say it was an accident, but I doubt that would be a good idea for me long term. I need to survive this class, no matter what.

"You nearly hurt her," Knox growls, sounding deadly. I move myself a little in front of Knox to protect poor Roger, but it does little as Knox just slides a hand around my waist and glares at Roger over my head. I'd have to jump a few times to break their eye contact and that would be pretty embarrassing. "I was inches away from breaking that pretty face of yours."

"I'm not an idiot; I wouldn't have gone too far," Roger replies, but Knox doesn't look the slightest bit impressed. Tavvy widens her eyes at me from Roger's side, and I shake my head. Men.

"Right, you all know the rules. We are going to continue the last class with the same partners. We all shall hope that Miss Dormiens can control her powers better this time," she says, and everyone laughs. I elbow Knox in the stomach, which only makes him and the others laugh more. Mr. Newman wordlessly stands at Miss A's side, watching me, and he isn't laughing. I really don't like that guy.

"I can," I feel I must add, and a few people laugh. Yeah, I should have stayed quiet.

"We all do hope so. Now get to it, class," Miss A demands, clapping her hands and making a sphere of water around her as she floats into the air.

"Come on, Madi. I will be easier on you than last time," Roger suggests, but I doubt it.

"You best be," Knox warns in a scary possessive tone before he walks away. I smile tightly at him before following Roger over to a clearing and standing on the marked areas.

"You ready for this, Madi?" Roger asks, parting his legs and placing his hands at his sides. Vines slide out of his hands, spreading to the floor as I smile and close my eyes.

"Yes." I call my power in the way that has become almost natural to me after helping Knox go to sleep. I might not be able to fight, but if anything touches me, I can use sleep to save myself. My nickname really is pretty useful. I open my eyes, feeling the warm dust on my hands that falls to the ground next to me as Roger sends a vine to slam into my stomach. I gasp as it knocks the air out of me, and I grab the vines as I fall to my knees. My dust spreads down the vines as Roger struggles to pull his vines away from my grip. In his panic, the other vine slams into my neck and wraps around, tightening as it lifts me into the air. I cry out in pain as my face slams into the roof of the building, the vines pressing me against the cold metal. I feel hot blood trickling down my cheek as I open my eyes, looking down at Roger who is staring right back. I know he wants me to let go, to grab the vine on my neck to save myself, but that isn't happening as more vines just replace the ones I pull off. I push past the fear and panic as I close my eyes, calling as much of my power as I can into the vines. I need to be free. I scream as power feels like it slams into every part of my body, and building up like a bomb as I keep my eyes locked on Roger's as he starts to look fearful, and for some reason, that makes me happy.

"Let her go! You are going to kill each other!" I hear Tavvy demand from a good distance away.

"We must see the winner," Miss A replies loudly, and my eyes crawl across to the left to see a wall of water all around us, blocking anyone from interfering. I pull my gaze to Roger just as my dust travels from the vines and hits his body. In an instant, his eyes close, and his body slumps to the floor. I fall quickly, almost in the blink of an eye, with the vines that are still tightly wrapped around my neck. I know nothing can catch me, and I was too high up. Tavvy was right, we are going to kill each other, but me first. My head hits the floor before my body does, my stretched arms grazing the floor as pain slams into my skull. The world blacks out into a dream that feels like a story I can't escape before I know it or can prevent it.

. . .

he dream comes on so quickly that I can't tell what is real as I pick myself up off the cold, frost-covered grass. I was in the gym, on the cold floor and not grass…wasn't I? Ravens quickly fly around me. They squawk loudly, the awful noise mixing with the harsh beating noise of their wings. I can't smell or hear anything else, I can't feel the cold weather that I can see around me. Thick snow starts to fall from the sky, dropping onto my bare shoulders as I see a person on the other side of the ravens. They part for him as he steps through, and my heart feels frozen as I stare at Quinton. My Quin, though he doesn't look like my Quin at all. He looks almost dead with pale skin, his black hair is longer and out of control, and he doesn't smile at me like Quin always does.

"Quinton?" I whisper, my breath coming out in puffs as the air must be cold, but I don't feel it.

"Danger. Danger. Danger," the ravens repeat again and again until I can only hold my hands to my ears as I fall to my knees, begging them to stop, but my voice is soundless.

"Madi…" I hear Quin say through the ravens, but soon he is lost, and there is nothing but cold, dead grass and screaming ravens as blackness takes over.

Chapter 21

Quin shouts my name, again and again as ravens rush around me, squawking and screaming. The sound is so painful, so never ending and all I want is for it to stop. It never does…

"Come on, Sleepy, you need to wake up now," I hear Sin whisper to me as his fingers slide through my hair and skim against my cheek. "Come back to me, baby."

"I'm going to get the healers again. She isn't waking up as they promised, and I'm concerned," Tobias shouts, and the slamming of a door makes me snap my eyes open in a rush, a deep gasp escaping my lips before I start coughing. Pain shoots down the one side of my head, reminding me in a rush of everything that happened. I glance at the white walls of the unfamiliar room, and the small bed I'm in with white sheets. There are curtains at each side of my bed which are pushed back, and they make me realise this must be a hospital of some sorts. I can feel my arms are wrapped up in bandages, and something is wrapped around my head. I'm sure I look a mess.

"Quin," I whisper as the dreams rush into my mind, even as I'm looking up at Sin who is leaning over me. He looks hurt for a second, but then it quickly changes to worry as he helps me sit up. Tavvy is sitting at the end of the bed, a relieved grin spreading across her face. Knox and Noah are in the room sitting in chairs, and they quickly rush over as I sit up.

"Did I win?" I ask, needing to know if it was all worth it.

"Roger passed out first, so yes, but you weren't the last one standing in class to win the prize though," Sin answers me, and the others just smile at me.

"Who won?" I ask, curious, but it doesn't matter. I wanted to prove to everyone and myself that I could beat Roger, even if I need to work on my falling game.

"I did," Tavvy says with a big smile, and I grin at her. "The brothers refused to fight and went with you to the medic bay, leaving only Ella and me as the strongest left. I beat her, so I finally won fight class!"

"You seem pretty happy I knocked myself out," I remark, though I am happy for her.

"Well...I was worried about you, but Miss A wouldn't let me leave class, so I made the most of it. At least one good thing came from it—I am going shopping, and I will get you a ballgown dress," she says happily.

"A ballgown dress for what?" I ask as Sin offers me a glass of water to drink as my voice is pretty croaky.

"The Lost Time Academy Ball, of course," Tavvy tells me. "I'm sure you can find yourself a date. It's in three months' time," she says very excitedly, and I can't help but smile at her, even though I'm not a fan of balls. I prefer secret parties and drinking, which I doubt this ball will have. I frown when my head hurts as I move to sit up more and place my hand on the lump covered by a bandage.

"How are you feeling?" Noah asks, gently picking up my other hand and holding it. He lifts my hand and kisses the back as he locks eyes with me. He doesn't seem to care that Knox and Sin are watching, and I can't even look at them to see their reactions.

"Just sore. I had a weird dream that felt so real," I explain to him. "The dream felt more than real. It was scarier than that fall from the ceiling."

"Another nightmare?" Tavvy asks, looking concerned.

"Nightmares?" Knox asks, and I remember that I haven't told them about my dreams yet.

"Yes, but this was different in a way I can't explain," I answer Tavvy and glance at Knox. "I have dreams and have done for a long time.

"Tell us about it, Sleepy," Sin lightly suggests.

"Every dream, there are crows, hundreds of them that circle me and squawk so loudly my ears hurt. The ground is always cold, but this time it was freezing, and snow was falling from the sky. That's not the strange thing though; this time, Quin was there. Quin walked through the crows that parted out of the way for him like he commanded them to do so. He didn't look like Quin though, he almost looked..." I drift off because I'm not sure how to even explain how he looked.

"Looked like what?" Sin asks.

"Dead. His skin was so pale that it had a tinge of blue to it. I'm scared for him, guys," I say, needing them to understand everything, because as much as I can tell them about the dream, I can't explain how worried and panicked it makes me feel. I can't explain how it felt to see Quin like that and not be able to just run to him, hold him close to me.

"We could ask our parents to look into how Quin is doing, if it would make you feel better," Knox suggests, but he is looking at Sin, who nods in agreement.

"Do you think the dreams could be real?" I ask them all. There is silence until Noah decides to answer me.

"Your power is sleep, and anytime you have dreams or nightmares, we should not ignore them," Noah says. "We never ignore our powers, it isn't right to do so. Our powers are there to protect us, and your dreams are likely warnings."

"Why would they warn me of Quin?" I ask, not understanding that.

"He knew you were with us, Sleepy. Remember?" Sin says, placing his hand on my shoulder. "I think there is more going on than we know about."

"Quin wouldn't ever hurt me. You all know that, you grew up with him as well!" I say, getting frustrated by their tone. Before any of them can say anything, Tobias walks into the room with a woman right behind him. The woman is dressed in a long white cloak that matches the rest of the room, and there is a white circle in the middle of her forehead.

"Now, now, all of you have class. As you can see, Miss Dormiens is awake, and I will let you know if she needs you all. Your teachers are waiting," the woman states, squaring up to them.

"We aren't leaving," Sin remarks.

"Go. I'm tired. I'm just going to rest anyway," I tell them, knowing I need some space and time alone to think about all of this and Quinton. I rest back, not looking at any of them as they leave the room, but Tavvy stays.

"You as well, little fairy," the healer demands. I feel Tavvy's hand on my shoulder a moment later, and I look up at her.

"They only tell the truth, but your dreams don't mean Quin is bad. They just mean Quin is clearly not just in your past," she tells me before she leaves the room. Quin isn't bad, he never was, and he never could be. The Tale brothers know this, and I just have to hope they don't find anything that says something different.

Chapter 22

"*N*ow, Miss Dormiens, which Master set up Lost Time Academy?" Mr. Newman, the professor of this class, decides to ask me as I doodle on my notepad, drawing a raven. For some reason, he always singles me out for questions, and over the last few weeks, I've noticed it more and more. Tobias, Tavvy and even Ella are in this class and would be much better to answer this, but oh no, he has to ask me. This class completely sucks in every way, and I don't have the answer, of course. I haven't gotten that far in the text book, even though I'm a hundred and fifty pages in. I'm sure Mr. Newman knows that, from the arsehole smile he is wearing.

"I know, sir," Ella states, holding her hand up in the air. Of course she does.

"Go on then, Miss Wateredge," Mr. Newman says, flashing a disappointed look my way as he talks.

"Master Tale, the very first of the Tale line, set up Lost Time Academy," Ella answers, and I quickly realise that must have been Tobias and Noah's ancestor. Even though Sin and Knox took the Tale name as children, they had other parents and different names before. They just never speak about it to anyone, and I'm not sure they even know much of their parents. A memory flashes into my mind as I look down at my book in front of me.

"*K*nox, what are you doing? We are all waiting outside for you to come back and play football," I breathlessly say after running around their big house to look for him. It's rare we come to their house, but their nanny made us food, and my parents said it was okay to come over. Knox is sitting in the kitchen, on a stool, but he doesn't look up at me. His hair is long, messy as it covers his face, but I hear the slight sob that escapes his lips. I run over, wrapping my arms around him. I've never hugged Knox before, not in the eight years we have known each other. He freezes for a second before hugging me back just as tightly, and he doesn't let go. Knox smells like peaches and chocolate, much like the ice creams his nanny gave us to eat.*

"No one ever hugs me...not even the new nanny because she says she is here temporarily, and hugs are for people who are permanent," he tells me.

"Is that why you're upset?" I ask, not letting go and hugging him tighter.

"No and yes. Everyone is temporary, and my parents aren't even our real parents. Last night, I found a letter that said Oisin and I are adopted," he tells me, and I had suspected something just because all the brothers are so close in age. Also Knox and Oisin don't look like Noah and Tobias's parents.

"No matter who your parents are, we are your family. Me, your brothers and Quin," I tell him, knowing it is true but slightly shocked from the knowledge. It doesn't matter though, they are all brothers even if they aren't blood-related. Knox looks up, still holding me closely, and smiles even though his lips are wet from tears.

"You won't leave me, will you, Madi?" he asks.

"Nope," I say and hug him once more, knowing I mean it. The Tale brothers and I are forever.

"*T*hat's correct. Now I want you all to continue to read your history books in your spare time, but the class is over," Mr. Newman States, and everyone swiftly grabs their things before starting to make their way out of class. I watch Tobias as he pushes through people to escape the class—or me. Either way, he is moving quickly enough that I'm going to struggle to catch up with him. I shove my book into my bag.

"Hey! I'm not just a book, I'm a person you know!" Lane complains as I do my bag up.

"It wasn't that bad," I mutter to him before sliding my bag onto my back.

"Where are you off to in a hurry?" Ella asks, and Tavvy simply blocks her view of me as I get out of the door. Tavvy is pretty awesome, and I really need to tell her that more often. I look around, searching for Tobias until I see him walking up the stairs. As quickly as I can, I slide past people and run up the stairs, following him as he goes to his own staircase and continues to walk up. I keep a good distance away as I follow him down the long corridor, well past his room, but he doesn't notice me either way. It soon becomes clear he is heading for the roof.

I wait for him to walk up the creaky stairs and open the door before running up them myself and catching the door just before it closes. I peek out to see Tobias standing near the edge of the roof, looking at the sun as it slowly sets in the sky. I peek my head out the gap further when he pulls something out of his pocket, a small black pouch. He picks out a glowing black rock, puts it into his mouth, then shivers before falling back onto his ass on the roof. It doesn't take an idiot to realise he just took some kind of drug; I just don't know what it is. I walk out, and Tobias looks my way, his eyes widening in shock.

"This is your secret then?" I say, walking over and sitting next to him. He looks pale, shaky and frankly a mess. "You are getting high on whatever that shit is?"

"What of it? We aren't kids anymore, Madi. I can do whatever the fuck I like," he tells me. "I don't need your judgement."

"And I'm not going to let you speak to me like that, you asshat. Our past doesn't mean you get to treat me like shit. If you want to spiral out of control and be fucking high all the time, I will leave you alone to do just that." I go to stand up, but he grabs my arm, and I look at him, seeing regret in his eyes, and it's enough to make me stop.

"Don't go," he asks me. "I'm sorry. I push everyone away, and I shouldn't do that with you. You are too close to me, too much for me to take in. You always were. If you will stay, I will tell you one secret."

"Just one?" I say, raising an eyebrow at him. He has me there, and he knows it.

"Don't be cheeky, Madi. Just one, and my brothers will kill me for telling you anything," he replies.

"I guess I could stay for a little bit," I say, grinning before sitting down next to him. He smells funny, like charcoal, and I quickly realise it must be the drugs. He can't focus on me as he looks my way, and all I want to do is slap the idiot for taking that shit.

"Thank you, Madi," he says and raises his bushy eyebrows, waiting for my question.

"Why were you arguing with Noah on that first day we saw each other again?" I ask him, knowing it's one of many questions I wish I could ask, but I only get one for now.

"I guess I promised to answer," he says and rubs his face with his shaky hands. "We came to the academy roughly a year ago, and within three days, our parents and the other Masters decided we would be engaged to marry Sophia Hedgeworth. She was a descendant of an old riddle, and she could sing anyone into doing anything. We all liked her, sort of. She was pretty and kind, but we all missed someone else too much to even let Sophia close. Knox let her closer than anyone else did, and it fucking haunts him."

I don't say anything because a deep part of me is jealous and another part of me is flattered. It's a funny feeling, and Tobias is too lost in his story to notice. "We agreed to at least be friends publicly, and we would deal with everything else later on. One night, we went to a party in the academy, and Sophia wanted to try moon rocks. I told her no, but she didn't listen and stole some anyway. I'm the only one who can take a high dosage of the stuff, and even a tiny amount of the rock would knock someone out. It killed her, and no matter what we tried, we couldn't save her. Noah blames me—hell, I blame me—and yet I can't fucking stop coming up here and getting more of this shit. I know I'm addicted to it, and it killed her...I'm a piece of trash for doing this."

"You're addicted to it, to your powers and this high you get from it. You need to stop, you know that, right?" I ask him, feeling sorry for them all. No wonder my Tale brothers are so messed up. I have to fix them or be there for them somehow.

"Yeah, I know it, Sleepy. It's like you stopping sleep though..." he tries to explain it to me. I reach up and brush away the black dust at the corner of his lip I can see, and he catches my hand. Very slowly, he slides my finger into his mouth and sucks off the dust. It shouldn't be sexy, and I should tell him no, but holy god, I'm going to hell as I don't stop him.

"Sleep doesn't kill me though, Tob," I gently remind him after clearing my throat and moving my hand away. "Or other people."

"I will try to stop," he tells me, but I don't believe him. Addicts always say that in movies, and they never stop. I know this isn't a movie, but I can't just let him do this alone.

"Let me help you. You don't have to go through this all alone, you know," I say, placing my hand on his shoulder. Tobias meets my eyes, as much as he can focus anyway with how high he is, and oh I want to believe him. Help him. I love Tobias, I always have done, and he knows it. I don't know how he feels about me though.

"Sleepy, my brothers tried to help and failed. What makes you think you could help me?" he asks. As much as the comment is a bit of an insult, I realise he is just pointing out a fact and trying to push me away again. He pushes everyone away.

"I'm far more stubborn than they are," I remind him, chuckling a little with him. The wind blows against us for a second, reminding us of where we are and how damn cold it is. I snuggle up to him, looking up at the cloudy sky. I wonder if it will snow soon, because it is cold enough to.

"I missed having you around. I forgot what it was like to be around you," he admits to me, resting his head over mine.

"I'm sure you've forgotten what it's like not to be high as a kite on moon rocks too. I'm not going anywhere, and neither are you. I want my guitar-playing Tobias back," I say, remembering how he used to sing songs to me as he played. I always told him that, one day, he will be playing on a stage because he is that good. Though I doubt that now.

"I haven't played since we left you and moved here. My dad smashed my guitar when I tried to play it instead of practice fighting," he explains to me. "I can't even sing anymore because my powers mix in with my voice, and it's not easy to control."

"I never liked that asshat," I admit, not knowing what else to say about the singing. I don't know his powers and what he can do.

"No one does," he replies with a tight smile.

"I'm going to fix you, you know that, right?" I ask, resting my head on his shoulder. "No more running away and avoiding me, Tob."

"You might be running from me instead," he warns. "I'm not safe for you."

"I never liked the safe boys."

Chapter 23

"Lane, if you are playing a joke on me again, I'm going to find scissors and start cutting some pages out," I warn him, because if I've learnt anything about Lane since we met, it's that he is a master prankster. In science class, we have to use our books to work out recipes and make crystals that we can later use to defend ourselves. I cringe as I remember my last few weeks that I spent working on a smoke crystal only for Lane to give me the wrong ingredient name, and it blew up in my face. "I spent days getting the black dust out of my hair last time you were sure adding that herb would work."

"I have apologised many a time for that little mistake," Lane remarks, but he is laughing, so it doesn't sound the least bit apologetic as I eye him.

Why did I get stuck with the most unhelpful book in history? I walk through the tables, slowing down when I see Noah and his perfect potion that he is picking crystals out of. His book is called Lady, which figures, and she is extremely helpful to all the brothers.

"Have you made yours yet?" Noah asks with a cheeky grin. "Would you like some help?" I stick my tongue out at him just as the classroom door is pushed open and Mr. Newman walks in, his eyes aiming straight at me.

"Miss Dormiens, you are called to meet the Masters," Mr. Newman explains, waving a hand at the open door. "Please come with me."

"What?" Noah exclaims, standing up. "Are my parents here?"

"Yes, but you are not called to see them, Mr. Tale," Mr. Newman responds. I pat Noah's shoulder as I pass him by, and shake my head.

"I will be alright on my own, and I will tell you everything later," I whisper to Noah, but it doesn't make him look any less concerned as I grab my book, shutting it with a smile at Lane and placing it in my bag as he grumbles. I chuck my bag over my shoulder before walking out the room, with Mr. Newman quick to catch up to my side as we head down the corridor towards the entrance hall.

"Where are we meeting the Masters then?" I ask Mr. Newman as we dodge a few students running to their classes.

"In the private meeting room which is only opened for Masters' visits. It is behind the dining room. This way," Mr. Newman instructs, never pausing in his large strides that I struggle to keep up with. We walk across the quiet entrance hall as I try to think of any reasons the Masters might want to meet with me, but I really have no clue. If I'm honest with myself, I'm nervous to see the brothers' parents again. It's been a long time.

"Why do they want to see me?" I ask Mr. Newman, because it is worth a shot, even if I don't like or trust him.

"You will soon see," he solemnly replies before we stop outside the dining room doors, and he pushes them open. I follow him in, and we walk through the space between the tables until we get to the back of the dining room where there are three doors. I've seen the cooks come in and out of the two doors on the right, but the left door I've never once seen opened. Mr. Newman knocks three times before pushing the door open and holding it for me to walk in. "If you don't already know, you must bow for a Master. Good luck."

I nod once at Mr. Newman before heading into

the room, which is deadly silent other than two hooded figures sat on the only chairs in the room. There's a circle pattern on the ground, and inside it has the cat tattoo thing, but this time the words "Lost Time Academy" are in English. Latin class isn't going well for me—or anyone in it, I suspect—so I'm happy to see some English around here. Both hooded figures lower their cloaks at the same time, revealing their stern expressions and familiar features that remind me of their sons. Mrs. and Mr. Tale. Mrs. Tale is the one in charge; you can see it in the way Mr. Tale looks to her for guidance and for her to speak first. The years have made her stern expression highlighted in wrinkles, and her hair is nearly all grey, the tips still slightly brown like her sons'. She lifts her head higher, a notion I can't help but notice. She thinks she is better than me, than anyone else, I suspect.

"Madilynn Dormiens, the last time we saw you, you were twelve years old and following my sons around like a lost puppy," she informs me, and I smile back at her as I reply.

"I like to think they followed me, not the other way around, Mrs. Tale," I tell her, and she frowns.

"Did they not tell you to bow in the presence of a Master? You are facing two of them," she says, somehow lifting her head higher and making her nose look bigger. I glance at Mr. Tale, who is completely grey-haired now, covered in stress wrinkles that gather a lot on his forehead. He doesn't look my way, instead he is focused on his hands like they hold all the answers in the world. The Tale brothers didn't get their love for breaking the rules from him, that's for sure. I'm actually hard pressed to see any similarities. When I pull my eyes back to Mrs. Tale, she looks extremely pissed. Well, I've already annoyed her, I might as well continue on this path. We were never going to be friends.

"I learnt you only bow for a queen, king or goddess. That is what my parents told me...are you any of those too?" I say, regretting it a little when she slides off her chair and storms over to me. She harshly slaps me around the face the moment she can, so hard that I trip a little but manage to hold myself up all the same. Mrs. Tale goes back to her seat, clearing her throat as I place my hand on my cheek, feeling hot blood dripping from the corner of my mouth. I wipe a thumb across it before steeling my back and meeting her gaze.

"I will ignore your impudence this one time, due to the mere fact you were a good friend to my sons. When we come face to face again, you will bow, Miss Dormiens, or I will break your back to make sure you do. Do you understand?" she asks, and I don't doubt her words. She would have to break me if she thinks I'm going to bow for her.

"I understand perfectly," I bite out, tasting blood on my lip that is feeling more swollen by the minute.

"Now, I called you here because we have fantastic news. The Masters' council has decided that you will be married," she says, a big smile on her red painted lips. Mrs. Tale feels like a snake in pretty clothing.

"To whom?" I immediately ask, feeling frightened for the first time since I came in here as her words register. Mrs. Tale knows it too, from the smile she is wearing.

"Mr. Roger Stalk. I believe you know of him," she replies, and my heart sinks almost instantly. Roger Stalk is not who I want to be with. Not now or ever. I'd rather throw myself off one of the large cliffs of this island than be forced into a marriage with someone I don't love. This isn't the middle ages, and she has to be crazy to expect me to just agree. Her sons won't agree, or at least I hope they wouldn't.

"What?" I whisper.

"Who else did you expect?" she asks and smiles before she laughs, because she knows the answer I won't admit to myself. "My sons? No, no. They will be engaged to Ella Wateredge who is a Master's child and only heir. They will make such lovely children with her, don't you think?" she says, pleased so much that it's a wonder her teeth don't pop out her mouth as she grins. I glance down at the tiled floor, seeing nothing but smooth, perfect flooring without a single crack. It's perfect, just like how Mrs. Tale expects her life to be. The Masters want complete silence and for us all to do what they want. Knox told me they are losing the war, and yet instead of defending us, they are spending their time planning arranged marriages by the sounds of it.

"No." The one word leaves my lips before I raise my head to meet Mrs. Tale's eyes that look so much like her sons'. This is risky of me, I'm too smart not to realise that, but I won't live a life where I'm commanded in everything I do. Mrs. Tale wants to take me away from the Tale brothers…and that isn't happening again. Ever. I've lost Quin, and I will not lose them too.

"No? I do hope you mean they wouldn't make lovely children and not that you protest about your engagement?" she asks, needing me to make it clearer, even though we both know what I mean.

"I won't marry Roger, or anyone that I don't choose myself," I slowly explain to her, making sure she understands me.

"Then you will be sent to the Masters' army, beaten until there is no personality left in you, and then you will die as a dark tale takes your pathetic life in the war," she replies, waving a hand.

"No wonder your sons always called you cruel and heartless. I feel sorry for Mr. Tale; at least your sons can escape you at times," I remark, and to my surprise Mr. Tale chuckles as Mrs. Tale goes a strange shade of red.

"Get out! Now!" she screams at me, and I smile tightly before pulling the door open and walking out. Even though I got to walk away, she still won the battle. I'm engaged...*how do I tell the Tale brothers that?*

Chapter 24

I quickly run up the stairs after Mr. Newman congratulated me on my engagement and I couldn't say a word in response to him. He looked very happy, too smug, and I was inches from wanting to punch him for that look. I don't look around or at anyone; I just run. I head straight for the only space I feel remotely safe in this place and the single place not all eyes are on me. The moment I step out into the cold air on the roof, I feel like I can finally breathe out the sob caught in the back of my throat. My cheek throbs and blood drips from where my teeth caught my lip when she hit me, but it's not the physical pain that makes me feel like I can't breathe. It's the dread and fear in my chest, the knowledge that I have no control over my life any longer. I was living a fairy tale, thinking that

I'd be given to the brothers and at least they would treat me right. I don't know Roger, nor do I like him from the time he spends kicking my ass in fight class. I wonder if Miss A knew all along we would be pushed together, so that's why for two months now, I've only fought him. At least I know I can put him to sleep easy if he pisses me off in our marriage. God, marriage. I'm seventeen, still in love with a human who haunts my dreams, falling for four brothers I was brought up with, and now engaged to another guy. What kind of fucked fairy tale is that?

"Madi?" I hear Sin call my name, and I gasp, realising that I have moved extremely close to the edge of the roof without realising it. "Whatever it is, whatever has happened, don't you dare jump. I swear I will follow you anywhere, even death."

"I wasn't going to jump," I turn to tell him and take a big step back. Knox, Tobias and Noah stand right behind Sin who comes to me first, placing his hand on my cheek, running his finger across the blood on my lip.

"Who hurt you?" Knox asks from my left, his voice just about concealing his fury. "Tell me a name."

"Your mum," I answer, clearly shocking them all. "She also told me I'm now engaged to Roger, and you guys are going to be engaged to Ella. I'm sure she will be a great fucking wife to you all." I push away from Sin, walking across the roof and not having the strength to turn back to them. I gasp as I look down at my hands, seeing them sparkling with dust that I wish could put me to sleep. My powers are too deeply connected to my emotions, the place in my soul that I have trouble separating the two.

"Don't you know by now that we can't be commanded to do anything?" Sin tells me, sounding close, but I don't look back. "And you are one of us. You always were, Madi."

"I don't care what the Masters tell us and what they expect. We are not their slaves, nor will we comply with their demands," Knox replies. "We are not theirs and neither are you. You are only ours."

"And we look after our own, we always have done. Madilynn Dormiens, you will not be controlled by anyone or be marrying someone you don't want," Noah remarks. "We don't play by the rules, and neither do you."

"Then they will send us all to the Masters' army where I don't know about you guys, but I will die," I say, trying to keep the sadness in my voice out. No matter what they say, it doesn't mean they have control over this entire world even if they don't play by the rules.

"Madi, we would never let you die or be forced to marry Roger, the plank," Tobias says, speaking for the first time, and I can't help but smile.

"Really?" I ask, turning to face them fully. I've not wanted to accept how much I care for each of them, how I would have been happy if Mrs. Tale said I was engaged to them all. I don't know when it happened, most likely before I even realised it, but I never want to be away from them all again. I don't want to play by the rules. I want to do whatever the hell I want, with the Tale brothers at my side.

"For now, we play along and keep our heads down. We can't tell you more, not without risking your life, but I promise you won't be marrying him. We won't be marrying Ella, and we have a plan to get us all out," Noah tells me, stepping closer and placing his hand on my cheek for a brief second before lowering it.

"And Tavvy. Tavvy doesn't deserve to be stuck here either," I add. If they have a way out, Tavvy has to be included. She has become as close as I imagine having a sister would feel like.

"Got it. Now, will you come here and possibly smile? I miss seeing it," Knox says, opening his arms for me. I run over and embrace him tightly, resting my head on his chest. I feel them all watching me even before I open my eyes.

"You are safe, Madi, and hardly powerless yourself. Always remember that," Tobias says, even though I really didn't expect him to say anything more.

"Knox, you stay with Madi. Brothers, we need to pay Roger a visit to make sure he understands that Madi is ours," Sin says, and damn he frightens even me with the possessive tone. Poor Roger. Then I remember Roger in fight class, being a dick and knocking me out whenever he gets the chance. He has this coming. Knox presses a protective kiss to my forehead as his brothers leave the roof, before looking down at me.

"I can heal that if you want?" he asks, nodding at my lip and cheek.

"No, don't. That would be hiding your parents behaviour when I want the world to see. They shouldn't just get away with what they like," I say, and Knox only nods. I know this must be hard for him, considering they adopted and brought him up.

"Want to escape this world for a little bit?" I don't question Knox, knowing I would trust him to take me anywhere, to any place. I trust him completely.

"Yes."

Chapter 25

"When you say 'escape this world', you mean literally?" I gape as Knox holds his hands in the air, his eyes closed and focused as blue light shines from his hands. The light stretches to the floor in a matter of moments, looking like a blue stand-up mirror, but the mirror shimmers almost like it is liquid. The outline is a bright white light, and Knox seems to be fine using this much power. It appears almost effortless for him. "I heard one of you could take people to other dimensions."

"Just me, and it is useful to beat my brothers in fight class. They can't fight me when they are stuck in another dimension," he explains, and I chuckle because that is pretty awesome. I never do get to see them fight, because I'm so focused on beating Roger that I don't notice what is going on around me. Roger beats me every time and knocks me out, or I beat him but still get knocked out. It's frustrating, but I'm getting quicker at using my powers every lesson. "Come with me. It's safe, I promise."

I slide my hand into Knox's and try to control my fear as he walks through the mirror first, and I follow straight through. I don't know what I expected to see, but this was certainly not it. It's a rainforest but not like any rainforest I've ever seen before. The trees tower into the sky, hiding the clouds as leaves fall from them in the wind. The leaves are light blue though, not green like a normal forest. We are in a clearing covered in white grass that is high enough to brush against my knees. A little in front of us is a wooden house, probably handmade, and right in front of it is a rock pool.

"It's safe, remember. I created everything here with my imagination, with my powers. It was just a field before, but now it's so much more," he explains to me. "Though I can only change things that exist here. Like trees, water and the very earth. Actually, this might not be earth, I'm not sure." I chuckle at that, leaning down slightly to run my fingers through the soft grass. This place smells seductive, like roses almost.

"You made all of this?" I turn and ask him, and

he grins as he holds his hand out. Out of nowhere, a flower slowly grows from a seed in his palm, stretching into a pretty pink rose. That is some sexy magic, the kind that would make any girl's knees feel weak. Knox smiles down at me as I stare at him, not the rose, noticing the changes in him recently. When I first got here, he was always tired, stressed, and there was never a smile on his lips. Now Knox is more relaxed with my help getting him to sleep, and just sometimes, I catch him looking at me, and he is so happy. As kids, I always used to love making Knox happy, because he had the best smile out of everyone I knew. Now that smile is a sexy smirk, which has the same effect—I always want to see it.

"For you," he says, offering me the flower after brushing it very slowly down the side of my cheek, not the one that hurts though.

"Ah, so you're the closet romantic," I say, swirling the rose around in my hand.

"No, that would be Sin," Knox says, walking past me and towards the house. I follow him over, passing the very tempting looking rock pool that I can feel the heat from, to the door of the house. Knox pushes it open and walks in, and I pause as I step in after him. The cabin is one large room where everything is made from vines and wood, and it is still very impressive. There are three sofas, with bases made of wood, and the fabric looks like giant blue petals.

"You want a drink, Madi?" Knox asks, and I turn to see him sat at the wooden bar, where rows of bottles line the counters behind him. "It's the only things I've brought into this place from the outside. You can't make beer and whiskey appear here. Sin wants to bring a TV in, but he hasn't worked out how to get electricity working."

"Everything is made from plants and trees. Is that the trick?" I ask, which makes a lot of sense. "Unless you bring in things."

"Yes, it's something to do with this place. I can go to another dimension where everything is made from metal. That place is boring though. I send Tobias there when he is too high and fucked up," he adds, looking frustrated. "I might have to send him there again soon."

"Is he still doing that stuff?" I ask, because I thought he was alright recently, and Knox shrugs.

"I think so, Sleepy," he despondently replies, clearly wishing he could tell me something different. Knox slides a beer in front of me after undoing the cap. I swallow the lump of disappointment in my chest, hoping that Knox is wrong about Tobias but knowing there is a good chance he isn't, as I take a long sip. I'm not a massive beer fan, but today has been stressful as hell, so anything will do. My lip stings from the cut, but I drink anyway, pushing past it.

"Tavvy says you guys sneak off all the time, and you just about confirmed that when you said the others were away on the night of the party. Where do you go?" I ask him.

"Secrets, Sleepy," he states, eyeing me carefully with that stubborn expression he shares with all his brothers.

"I'm tired of secrets and lies. I don't want to hear them anymore," I say, placing the bottle down. "You said I'm one of you, and that means you can trust me, right?"

"I know you are one of us. You know it too, but sometimes secrets are there to keep you safe," he warns me, but it doesn't scare me all that much. I'm already scared of this world; it's fucking terrifying and we all know it. The problem is, I want more than just surviving. I want to live, to fall in love with the men close to me. The kind of love that makes me not fear death as much as I fear losing any of them. We have all been on the edge of this for so long, just inches away before they left. I just started to fall for each of them then, and now it's worse than before. It feels like my soul is burning when I'm around them. And all I do is keep the fire going because it's better than nothing. It's better than a life without the Tale brothers in it.

"I'm starting to think there is nowhere safe when it comes to this world I've just been thrown in," I decide to say, rather than anything I'm thinking. My thoughts aren't safe around them, I'd end up blurting too much out.

"We do work for our parents, missions of importance..." he pauses for me to take that in. "The dark tales are changing leadership, and their armies are not attacking any longer. There is something going on, and we are keeping close watch."

"That's dangerous," I say, feeling my heart beating quicker at the thought of them being around dark tales, let alone spying on them.

"Very, but we can escape in a moment's notice to here. We aren't really in danger," he replies, after taking a long sip of his beer. "That's why they ask us to go."

"The other night, they didn't have you there, so how would they have escaped?" I enquire.

"As usual, nothing escapes you, Madi. Right, well, that night wasn't a mission, that was our parents calling us to a meeting to 'tell' us of our engagement with Ella," he explains to me, and for a second, I feel too shocked to actually move. *They knew all this time.*

"You've known this whole time," I say, placing my drink down and walking away from the bar towards the door. I want to leave. "You all knew and didn't tell me. You all say I'm one of you, but clearly not. You guys have your secrets, and I'm firmly on the outside."

"We don't care about Ella. Neither should you," Knox firmly says, putting his own drink down, I notice out of the corner of my eye. "And you are not on the outside."

"Of course I care about your engagement, and all these secrets mean I must be someone you can't trust! That is the problem!" I exclaim, spinning around and freezing when I see Knox is right behind me. Before I know it, his lips are on mine, his hands are in my hair, tugging me closer. Knox kisses me slowly, taking his time to explore every part of my lips before deepening the kiss. I know this is a kiss I could never forget, just like I could never forget Knox himself. I'm speechless when he pulls away, and I know it was only a little kiss; it just felt so much more.

"We don't care, because she is nobody, nothing, compared to how we feel about you. We wouldn't fight for her, we wouldn't touch her, and there is only one girl in this entire fucked up world that we all want. Madi, if it isn't obvious by now, that girl is you," he tells me, his finger drifting slowly down my neck to my shoulders.

"You are romantic, you know that," I mutter, not having a clue what to say.

"Only with you, Sleepy," he replies and kisses me softly one more time before letting me go. "You've had a difficult day. Let's just relax for a bit," he suggests, offering me a hand. After getting our drinks, we sit on the sofa, cuddled up, and spend the rest of the day talking about the past. Knox was right, this was just what I needed.

Chapter 26

"*D*id you expect to have this many men in your life, Madi?" Tavvy asks as I pull on my clothes and glare up at her as she lies back in her top bunk. "One fiancé that is shit scared of going anywhere near you, four hot as hell brothers that have always been in love with you, and one creepy ass floating man head in your book. It certainly all adds up."

"I'm pretty sure my dad would have a meltdown if he realised how many men I have in my life. I'm sure he'd prefer you for a daughter in law," I honestly say, even though the Tales laws are shit and ban relationships that aren't chosen. It's ridiculous if you ask me, and I have no intention of marrying Roger Stalk. Though any time I've seen him this week, he has literally turned around and run in the opposite direction. Whatever the Tale brothers said freaked him out. Their possessive nature shouldn't be sexy, but holy hell, it is.

"The Tale brothers aren't that bad," Tavvy remarks with a low chuckle. *Oh, they are and she knows it.*

"Dad never liked them," I point out. I'm pretty sure his warning not to trust anyone was meant for the Tale brothers. He'd have a meltdown if he learnt I was back to being friends with them all the time. I think we are friends...that kiss sometimes. I've only kissed Sin and Knox...but that's bad enough on its own. I'm always thinking about Noah and Tobias when I'm not replaying my kisses with their brothers. I'm also not over Quinton, not one little bit, as I'm always thinking of him as well, and then I don't know how I would choose one of them. This is pretty complicated.

"Actually, I'm not surprised. My dad wouldn't be a fan of four sexy and dangerous men in my life," she says and then sighs. "Though I would *not* be opposed."

"I had five, remember? Quinton was always there, and dad hated him the most. I never knew why," I remind her, needing to add Quinton's name to this conversation. I look at the pillow, feeling like it burns a hole into my hand and begs me to call him. *He asked me not to call him, remember, Madi?*

"Most likely because he is human," she says, and I can hear the sympathy in her voice. I finish pulling my shoes on just as the door is knocked a few times. "See you later, Madi. Don't do anything I wouldn't do with sexy Noah."

"That doesn't leave much left not to do," I quip with a laugh following my words, and she throws a pillow at me, which I just dodge out of the way of before pulling the door open to see a beaming Noah leaning against the door frame.

"Morning, beautiful," Noah says, running his eyes over me and winking before looking up at Tavvy in bed. "Hey, Tavvy."

"Hey, I'm beautiful too!" Tavvy mutters.

"You know you are. See you later, Tavvy," I say, laughing with Noah as we leave the room, and I shut the door behind us. I cross my arms, wishing I pulled a hoodie on because it is damn cold out these days. There is no snow, but I'm still waiting to see some fall.

"I know we usually do practice fighting on Sundays, but the gym is empty tonight, and it's a good idea to practice before fight class tomorrow.

Roger is sick, so you will be teamed against someone new," he explains to me. "And I want to make sure you can defend yourself in close combat."

"What is Roger sick with?" I ask. I didn't think Tales could get sick like humans. We heal too fast, so viruses cannot bring us down for much longer than an hour. I read that somewhere in the ridiculous amount of homework I have.

"A broken rib and nose. Don't worry about it," Noah waves off my wide-eyed look.

"Who did that to him?" I demand, stopping at the top of the stairs as he walks down a few steps and stops to look back up at me with a sheepish expression.

"Roger said something he shouldn't have about you, and he needed to learn a lesson. Trust us, Madi," he says, coming to stand in front of me and reaching for my hand. "It's nothing major, and he will be good as new in a few days, thanks to the nurse at the medic bay."

"Do I have a choice but to trust you?" I ask, linking our fingers together and sighing.

"Yes, but you know you do anyway," he reminds me, leading me back down the stairs together. We head straight to the gym, where Noah opens the door and lets me in first. The lights are already on, and there are mats all over the floors.

"We've had six lessons now, and I've been gentle with the close combat. I feel you need to learn how to trust your instincts," he explains to me.

"How am I meant to do that?" I ask.

"In the same way you trust your powers to protect you, you need to learn to trust your instincts. We aren't human, nor do we have their instincts. We are supernaturals, with increased strength and senses. Those senses keep us alive more than our powers ever could," he explains to me. I guess it makes sense. I should have had serious injuries from the amount of times Roger has dropped me from the ceiling or thrown me into walls at this point.

"I don't understand how to use those," I reply, because seriously, I don't.

"That's what I'm here for," he says and pulls out a long piece of black fabric from his pocket.

"You are going to blindfold me?" I nervously ask, stepping back.

"Yes, and then you are going to defend yourself from my attacks," he replies, a playful glint in his eyes. He is liking this way too much.

"I can't do that. I'm just going to end up in bruises," I say, shaking my head. I'm not some secret ninja, and there is only one thing that will happen if he attacks while I can't see, and that is my butt getting hurt.

"You can and will. Don't worry, you just need to trust me and yourself," he says, holding the blind-fold up. I eye him carefully, knowing I don't have a massive choice in this. I nod once, trusting Noah to guide me even when I can't see a single thing. Noah walks behind me, placing the blindfold over my head, and I hold it in place for him as he ties it up. After he finishes tying the blindfold, he steps away, leaving me alone. The odd thing is I don't hear him walk away, he is silent like a cat.

"Focus," Noah warns me, and I squeal when what feels like a ball flies into my thigh. I know it's a sphere of light that Noah can make as he's used it to train me before. It doesn't burn; it just feels warm. I spin around, placing my hands out and trying to see where he's going to send the next one from. A second later, my arm is hit, and I jump backwards. I don't know how long this goes on for, but after a while, I hold my hands up in the air.

"Enough! I give up," I protest, rubbing some of the sore areas he hit twice.

"If I were a dark tale, I would have killed you by now, and you can't give up. We don't give up, Madi. Now focus," he demands and throws a ball of light right into my ass. "Tobias gives up, he always does, and it drives me crazy. Like right now, he has disappeared again, most likely high. You are not Tobias, and you are not giving up already." I try to ignore the instant worry about Tobias and the fear I can sense in Noah's voice, but it's not easy. Dammit, Tobias. When he reappears, I'm knocking his ass out and getting Knox to throw him in the other dimension.

"Stop throwing them at my butt!" I shout at him, and I only hear him laugh in response. Right, I need to focus. Maybe I should call my power and just not use it? When I call my powers, it's like a wave of cold water is thrown on my body, and it makes me focus in a way that I'm not usually focused. Maybe that's what Noah means. I lower my hands to my sides, flattening my palms against my thighs in case I call dust by accident. I find the source of my power, and it instantly washes over me, making me more aware of everything, of every part of my body and my surroundings. The world seems to freeze for a second, and then I hear it. Something coming towards me. I spin around slamming my hand into whatever was aimed at me. The sphere of light crashes into my hand and disappears without hurting me.

"Impressive. See, Madi? You can do this. Now

let's continue this for a few hours." I smile and nod my head, before letting my powers take over. I think I'm finally getting good at this "being a little different" thing. Hopefully, I'm good enough to keep myself alive.

Chapter 27

"*A*re you excited to see who she puts you against today?" Tavvy asks as we run, getting near to the end of the last lap. At least I'm not completely out of breath now. After all this running, I'm slowly getting used to it—*slowly* being the key word there. I'd happily stay in bed, dreaming of Doritos, which I miss so much.

"I'm excited that Miss A isn't chasing us today because she is too busy chatting with Mr. Newman. That's about it," I reply to Tavvy, glancing quickly over to see Miss A laughing with her hand on Mr. Newman's shoulder. They are definitely dating or something, not that I know if Miss A is engaged or ever has been. She is still "Miss," so I doubt it. Maybe teaching is a profession that means you don't have to get married or something. I will ask about that later, because at this point, I'm happy to teach my whole life away rather than be forced to marry anyone.

"Come on, smile, you might be against me!" Tavvy says with a creepy happy grin.

"Considering you are a badass, and I know you well enough to know you won't take it easy on me, I'm not wishing for that," I reply to her.

"True. Plus, I like kicking Ella's ass," Tavvy says, winking at me. I laugh, a breathless laugh as we get to the end of the lap and stop. We get to wait a few moments before Miss A calls us all over to gather around her. I go to stand next to Knox just as the main door slams open and Tobias falls into the room, just about managing to stop himself from falling flat on his face. Tobias grins, pushing his hair out of his eyes as he walks over, swaying as he struggles to stay standing. He is high again, just like Noah suspected.

"Who is fighting me today then?" Tobias shouts, just as he gets to my side and wraps an arm around my shoulder. He stinks of women's perfume, and there is lipstick on his neck. Tobias also has black dust around his lips and nose. Overall, he looks a fucking mess, and I put my hand up before his brothers can say anything. I don't know if it's jealousy or anger that makes me want to fight him, but it sure isn't that I feel sorry for Tobias.

"I will."

"Fuck no, Madi," Knox interrupts, storming over to me, but Miss A places a wall of water around Tobias and me, blocking him. Knox glares at her then at me, and I shake my head. Noah and Sin look between each other before giving me a nod, letting me do this.

"Madi and Tobias, fight fair, and whoever wins may have the rest of the day off," Miss A states, and I nod at her, walking back a few paces as Miss A keeps all the students on the other side of the wall, making sure they can't interrupt. I can't look at them, so I keep my focus on Tobias instead. I need to win this, to show them I'm not weak and to knock Tobias out so he can sleep this off. If his brothers do this, then he will get hurt, and that isn't going to help anyone. I stare into Tobias's dark brown eyes, seeing the silver specks in them that I've always loved.

"Do you know what powers I have, Sleepy?" Tobias asks as we start circling each other, though he is moving slowly. He is making this too easy.

"No. Something to do with the moon," I reply as his hands start to glow white. "I assume it's more than just making your drugs so you can forget everything."

"It is," he tightly replies and smiles widely. I cry out as pain slams into my head for only a moment before it fades. I look up to see Tobias holding his hand out, which is glowing a silver colour. The silver glow is spreading from his hand like string, and it is tightly wrapping itself around my wrist.

"You will stand up, and then slowly dance your way to me," Tobias whispers into my mind, and my legs lift me up without me even realising it. My arms lift above my head, swaying as my hips move to an unknown beat that plays in my head. I scream in my head as I get closer to Tobias, who is curling a finger towards me, the silver string spreading all over my body like rope. I hear his brothers shouting at me, Tavvy is shouting something too, but I can't hear their words. I can't hear anything but Tobias and the lure he whispers into my mind. I get closer and closer until I'm right in front of him. He smirks happily, like this is all over. It isn't.

"Now kiss me," he whispers.

"NO!" I scream in my head, pushing my own powers to my hands, with all the strength I can possibly gather. I lift my one hand the moment the silver string falls to the floor, his control fading, and Tobias is gaping at me in shock. *I won't be forced to do anything.* Before he can make a countermove, I punch Tobias hard in the face, dust blasting out of my hand. He falls backwards, collapsing to the floor with a loud thud as my knuckles sting. *Thank you, Noah, for teaching me how to punch.*

"Well done, Miss Dormiens." Miss A claps and the whole class cheers my name. I stare down at Tobias as Tavvy gets to my side first, followed by Knox, Sin and Noah.

"I don't have a clue how you did that, but man, it was sexy," Sin tells me and winks at me when I look up at him. A smile tilts my lips up, even when I'm worried about Tobias.

"What are we going to do about him?" I ask no one in particular.

"I don't know...but he deserved that punch. Maybe it will knock some god damn sense into him. Sin, help me carry him back to our room where he can sleep it off," Knox says. I link my hand with Noah as we watch Knox and Sin carry Tobias out the room. I can't help but wonder if anything is going to be enough to stop Tobias from getting high on moon rocks when it's linked to his powers. Maybe nothing anyone can do will make him forget. *Maybe I'm too late to save him.*

Chapter 28

"No way, he can really do that?" I whisper to Noah who is sat at my side as we both stare across the dinner hall at a boy Noah promises can stretch any part of his body and change his body into any animal as well. It's crazy to think all these teenagers can do a million different things, and I'm learning how to use my own power. I only wish the damn dreams of ravens and Quin would stop. I'm pretty tired all the time, thanks to them. It makes me miss Quin and feel guilty for my...well, whatever it is with the Tale brothers.

"I've heard Ella likes to visit him because he can stretch something down below," Tavvy adds in, waggling her eyebrows at me. I laugh with the guys who shake their heads at me, all of them except for

Tobias who is still in his room after fight class yesterday. I feel guilty for hurting him, but I'm more concerned with why he took the drugs this time, since he was trying to stop. Guilt is a funny thing, something I've only had to feel once or twice over simple things I did wrong. Tobias thinks that he killed his fiancé and that it is all his fault. I understand why he would want to forget the world, but not this way.

"Did you say my name?" Ella asks, stopping right behind my seat. *Speak of the devil.* I turn my head back to see Ella glaring down at me, her long red hair covering her shoulders. That's all of her body that is covered though, considering she has a tiny tube top on and skinny jeans that barely cover her hips, let alone her ass. It makes me wonder if she is shopping for the wrong size or just wants to look like this. It's most likely option two.

"Yes. Now go away," Tavvy suggests, shooing her with her hand before tucking into her food, pretending Ella has taken her advice, which of course she has not.

"Ella, what do you want?" I ask her as she leans over the table, blocking my view of Noah. Her long red hair falls into my face, making me lean back in my seat.

"You may fuck them now, new girl, but it will be

my bed they will all be in at the end of the year. They are engaged to me, not you. The Masters just told me," she says, a smug expression on her pretty face.

I push out my chair, ignoring Tavvy and the brothers' advice to ignore her. The dining room goes deathly silent, and a few people run out the room just in case. Ella only backs up, crossing her arms with that stupid smug look.

"They aren't marrying you, dumbass," I remark, watching how red she goes, almost the colour of her hair.

"They are! You have a fiancé, so why don't you leave mine alone!" she shouts at me, pointing a long red-nailed finger into my chest. I push her away, and she steps back, huffing before looking at the brothers. "Aren't you going to defend your fiancé?"

"No." Knox is the only one to reply, and it's a tense reply at that. It makes Ella look even more embarrassed.

"Just leave them the hell alone, you whore!" Ella screams in frustration. *This is a real shame, I was starting to think we could be friends.*

"Make me," I suggest, and she almost sweetly smiles before running and slamming herself into me. We fall to the floor, and before she can do anything, I grab her hair, pulling tight as I wrap my legs around her waist. She screams, pushing me away as I call my power and push my hand into her face, feeling warm dust on it. Her hands tighten on my neck for a second before Ella collapses with wide eyes, her head banging into my shoulder with a puff of dust that makes me cough. I look over her to see Knox standing over us, shaking his head with his arms crossed. Noah, Sin and Tavvy are laughing their heads off though. All I can think of is how Ella is damn heavy.

"What is going on in here!" Miss Noa's strict voice beckons across the dining room, and I quickly push Ella's passed out body off me and crawl to my feet. I look over to see Miss Noa place her hand on the ground, her eyes going white for a moment before she straightens up.

"Miss Dormiens, I did not expect you to be such a troublemaker," she remarks and looks behind me. "Mr. Tale, any of you actually, can take Miss Wateredge to the medic bay. Make sure the healer informs her when she wakes up that she has detention tomorrow night."

"I got this," Knox says, picking Ella up like a sack of potatoes and carrying her out of the room.

"As for you, Miss Dormiens, I will see you in

detention tomorrow," she says, and I have a feeling I'm not going to like detention, nor is it going to be like detention at my human school when I could just run out when the teacher wasn't looking. I should have at least slapped Ella, then this detention would have been worth it.

Chapter 29

"*G*ood luck," Tavvy whispers to me as I pull the door open and glance back at her. "It can't be as bad as you are thinking."

"I don't trust this school, and either way, I'm going to be stuck alone with Ella for hours," I whine.

"Don't kill her," she says with a chuckle, before snuggling back into her bed. I look longingly at my own bed before leaving the room, knowing it is just best to get this all over with. Detention is going to be bad, no matter how much I try to put it off. I cross my arms against my chest, thankful I have my comfy hoodie on and my favourite joggers. At least I will be comfy during this torture. I get to the top of the stairs, where Ella and Miss Noa are waiting for me. I walk down, pausing as Knox, Sin, Noah, and more to my surprise, Tobias walk over.

"Miss Dormiens and Mr. Tale, all of you are late," Miss Noa tuts, and Ella keeps her glare firmly fixed on me as she tugs at the casual clothes she has on. It must feel weird for her to wear actual clothes. I frown at the Tale brothers before placing my hands on my hips, waiting for an explanation. Noah comes over first, wrapping his arm around my waist.

"We made a mess in the science lab and got detention. Shame that," Sin states and fist bumps Noah.

"You all got detention on purpose to spend time with me?" I ask, because that is pretty romantic, if you ask me.

"You guys are all sickly sweet about her," Ella huffs, flipping her hair over her shoulder as Miss Noa clears her throat. We all follow after her as she takes us behind the staircase and unlocks a rusty door. After a few pushes, the door creaks open, and Miss Noa wipes the cobwebs away that cover the door. Ella makes a disgusted sound and steps back, wiping her arms like the spiders are on her or something. Miss Noa brushes the wall of dust, finding a switch, and clicks it on. Dozens of wall lights switch on one after another all the way down the staircase.

Miss Noa starts walking down, and I follow after her, hearing the guys and I'm sure Ella after us.

"This is the old library, which has been out of order for many terms. We want to clean it up and get it back to its original way. Your detention is to spend three hours cleaning and dusting all the books," Miss Noa explains.

"God, someone save me," I hear Ella mutter, making me smile as we get to the last step and into the big stone room. There are dozens of boxes, covered in white sheets, littering the room. All the walls have bookcases with no books in, and there is a large statue of two women with benches around them. The women are made of white stone, which is carved to show off their long dresses and very long hair. The women are holding each other's hands, looking up at the ceiling and the light right above them.

"The statue is of the goddess that made our kind. Both the sisters," she tells me, and I look at their faces, wondering if they would even care about the war they created. Their children who are fighting it every day.

"What about the goddess that made humans and gave life to the world?" I ask her, because she started all of this, so surely she should be the one in the middle of the sisters.

"We do not know who made the statue or how old it is, so I have no clue why there aren't three sisters in the sculpture," Miss Noa explains to me, though she seems sad about it. "Now, I am going to lock you in here, and I will be back later. If you mess around and do not work, you will all be back here tomorrow night." We are all silent for a moment as Miss Noa walks back up the steps and slams the creaky door shut, turning the lock.

"Right, girls open the boxes and clean the books with the dusters. We will start lifting the heavy ones and bring them over to you. Then put the books away," Noah makes a plan, clapping his hands once and dust goes everywhere in a puff, making us cough.

"Sounds good," Knox says, stepping over some boxes and going to the big pile of them in the back.

"I'm going to pull the sheets off everything and give the girls some to dust with before joining you," Tobias says, flashing me a guilty and sad look. I want to say something, but I'm not sure what. The last thing I did was punch him in the face while he was high as a kite. It's pretty awkward between us and I'm still waiting for an apology I doubt I'm getting. Tobias never did say sorry, not ever as kids or teenagers.

"Why don't we sit on the benches, there is

enough of them, and start opening boxes?" I suggest to Ella, because we might as well use the only seats in here.

"Fine, new girl," Ella mutters, following me over to the benches. I sit down on one, and Ella chooses to sit next to me.

"I've been here a while now, I'm not that new," I remark, pulling a box closer and ripping the tape off.

"There hasn't been anyone newer than you, so yes you are," Ella replies, getting her own box. We silently go through about five boxes, piling books up and dusting them with the cloth that Tobias brought us.

"They love you, don't they?" Ella quietly asks.

"I don't know. We don't talk about things...we just have each other. It's complicated, Ella," I honestly tell her. As much as I don't like it, we are all linked together for a little while. There is no point lying to her.

"I'm sorry for what I said and the fight. I'm sorry for going after them. I know it's pointless and they will never listen to the rules anyway, not when you are around. As much as I'd like to marry those sexy guys, I would hate it if it were a marriage just on paper. I can't make the Masters change, but your Tale brothers might stand a chance," she says, sounding like an honest and nice person for the first time since we met.

"Thank you for saying that," I reply, somewhat speechless. I didn't expect her to say anything.

"This doesn't mean I like you or we are friends," she reminds me. "We are just a step above enemies."

"Got it," I reply, smiling at her, and she smiles back for a moment before turning away. Maybe Ella isn't all bad after all.

"Everyone, come and look at this!" Sin shouts over from somewhere behind us.

"I'm not seeing anything. This place is yuck," Ella says when I get up and look down at her. I shake my head and step over the piles of books and head to the back of the library where Sin is kneeling down, looking at the floor where a box has broken and spilled out the contents on the floor. Knox, Tobias and Noah get to my side when I get closer, seeing the box was full of shiny daggers with jewels on them. I pick one up with a blue gemstone in the hilt, and I hold it up in the light.

"Do you think Miss Noa knows these are down here?" Noah asks, eyeing up the yellow stone dagger he has picked up.

"No way. These look old, and they should be in the Tale's castle with the Masters' protection,"

Knox replies, his eyes fixed on the green stone dagger.

"There are six of them, maybe we should keep one. Even Ella," I reply as the guys pick up their own ones. Each one has a different coloured gem, and the last one on the floor has a red gemstone in it.

"You want to give one to Ella?" Sin asks, not hiding his shock.

"We have come to an agreement. It doesn't mean I won't kill her if she does any of you, but for now, we are good," I explain, freezing when I realise what I just said.

"You sound like you are making a claim on us, Madi," Sin teases, though it isn't all a teasing question. They look at me seriously, like they want an answer.

"I-I didn't mean—" I nervously start to mumble out.

"We are playing with you, Sleepy." Knox puts me out of my misery, and I sigh. I'm not ready to talk about whatever is going on between us, and neither are they, I suspect. "Go on, give Ella her new gift." I smile at him before turning around, but Noah stops me with one question.

"Madi, will you be our date to the ball? For all four of us?"

I turn around, seeing them all waiting for an answer, even Tobias who looks more nervous than the rest of them. He should be nervous, and I'm not forgiving him until I get the sorry I want.

"Yes," I simply answer, because there is no one else I would go with. I walk away before they can say anything else, and for the first time, I'm excited to go to the ball.

Chapter 30

"*I*t's beautiful, and I can't believe you just bought it for me," I whisper, spinning around in the long, light blue dress that is lacy at the top. The material is soft and fits me perfectly. The bottom is layers and layers of blue fabric that gather together. Around my waist is a thick piece of material that is tied in a bow at my lower back. The top half of my back is exposed with lacy sides holding it up. I've never worn anything this nice or expensive. I've told Tavvy a million times over that I'll pay her back, but she won't have it. I look behind me as Tavvy finishes curling one last strand of my long hair, letting it freely fall down my back and around my shoulders. If I were blonde, I'd sure look like Sleeping Beauty in this dress.

"My family is one of the richest in the tale

community, so don't worry about me spending my dad's money. He is a lawyer who makes sure no human ever wants to speak about our kind if they find out. Our dust can make people do anything we demand," she explains to me, and I didn't know any of that. Tavvy doesn't talk much about her parents, and I got the impression she wasn't close to them when she would prefer a shopping trip rather than a phone call to home. "That's how he got so rich. My mum doesn't have descendant powers from her line, but she can talk anyone into anything either way. They are a cool power couple."

"That's a cool power, Tavvy, and thank you," I turn back and tell her. Tavvy has a stunning green dress on that hugs her curves, with a long split up to her upper thigh. The green material is shiny but almost has a glitter shimmer to it as she moves. Tavvy's blonde hair is up in a bun, surrounded by plaits she has woven in.

"Don't thank me, just enjoy your night," she says, winking. I hold my arm out for her, and she links her arm through mine as we leave our room. I try not to trip in the slight heels Tavvy got me, but I'm walking a little strangely, I think. Tavvy has ridiculously high heels on, making her so much taller than I am. She doesn't have a date, and I still remember her answer when I asked her who she was going with. It went along the lines of, "I don't need a man, and if I want a date, I'd pick them. No one in this school could handle me," and honestly, she is right. Tavvy needs a special kind of person to keep up with her. I even struggle to just as her friend. We get to the end of our corridor just as Ella and a blonde-haired guy walk past us. Ella has a short, very tight and glittery black dress on with killer heels. It looks stunning with her long red hair falling in waves. Ella smiles at me briefly, but then sharply looks away.

"I can't believe you guys are kind of friends now," Tavvy whispers to me as we head towards the stairs, where I can hear light music coming from somewhere, and the stairs themselves are lit up with floating, multicoloured lights.

"Under all the snarky bad attitude, there is a good person. I see it, don't you?" I reply, because honestly, that's how I see Ella. I don't know her parents, but Masters as parents can't be easy. The Tale brothers struggled growing up and have to deal with their own. I think Ella is a bitch because she was brought up to be one, to not show weakness, I suspect. Under it all, I think she is pretty nice.

"If you say so," Tavvy says, shaking her head at me. We walk down the stairs behind another group of students and follow them through to the dining hall, which has been transformed into a room I just about recognise. The floor shimmers like silver liquid filled with glitter, yet it is hard as stone to walk on. The ceiling is filled with dozens of floating spheres, which slowly let hundreds of tiny droplets of light fall from them. In the corner, instruments play music, though there is no one actually playing them. On the other side, where food is usually served, are tables filled with drinks and snacks, with teachers behind them, handing things out.

I look back into the room to search for my Tale brothers when they find me. They all stand a few feet away, dressed up in tuxes that make them look dangerously attractive. My mouth goes dry as they walk towards me, and I have to pinch myself because there is no way guys as hot as the Tale brothers are looking at me like this. I'm so used to them, I forget what it is like to really see them. They are imposing, strong, and everything you could want to see in front of you. The Tale brothers are everything.

"Madi, you look gorgeous," Sin speaks first, and I'm still too speechless to reply to him before he carries on speaking. "Can I steal you for a dance?"

"Come on, guys, why don't we get some drinks and spike them? This party needs a dose of fun,"

Tavvy says as I can only nod once at Sin, agreeing to dance. Sin doesn't need any more of an invitation to take my hand, leading me into the dancers. He grins as he pulls me into his arms in the middle of the crowd that parts to give us our own space. Sin leads the dance, keeping my body pressed against his and my hands resting on the back of his neck. I don't notice the well-played music, the way Sin moves my hips to the beat, never missing a step as we spin around; I only notice how he looks down at me.

"This place is magical, almost unbelievable, if I'm honest," I say, needing to break the tension and say something. Anything.

"Before I knew the truth, fairy tales and happy endings seemed unbelievable. Now they are real. Magic is real, and despite everything bad about this world, it makes us special and ever so lucky," he replies, pulling me closer and pressing his warm lips to my forehead. I close my eyes, breathing in how Sin smells like home and everything that feels safe.

"Magic is frightening...but you are right, it is special. We are lucky," I reply to him.

"I hope to one day live in a world where dark tales don't exist and we can be safe. Maybe we can all live together in a house, have a few children, and be happy until we die," he tells me, being so shockingly honest that I'm not sure how to respond to it.

"Sounds like you have it all planned out," I nervously reply. I haven't thought about a future for us all, I don't even know where to start. Sin leans back, and slides a hand under my chin, never stopping our dance as he stares down at me.

"I want a future with you, that is my only plan, Madi," he explains to me, and as I stare into his light silver eyes that are as enchanting as he is, I want the same. I've always wanted the same, and we have a chance at that future now. I lean up and gently press my lips to his, needing to kiss him. Words aren't always the best tool to tell someone how you feel, a kiss can do so much more. A scream makes us jolt apart only seconds before a powerful explosion slams into the side of the dining room, and the wall blasts into a million pieces. I cover my eyes, and when I open them, the teachers are standing in a line, blocking us from seeing what is in front of them.

"Students, run into the forest to the portals!" Miss Ona turns back to shout at us, locking her eyes with me for just a moment, and there is fear. So much fear in them. Sin grabs my hand, dragging me through the students running for the door. The students in front of us scream at something I can't see, and Sin rapidly turns us around. We run to the back of the dining hall, where the door is already open. I grab the door frame, stopping Sin from dragging me, to look back. Knox and Tobias are fighting two men who have incredible powers. Knox is spinning fire, water and lighting in circles around the men while Tobias is using his powers to make the men walk into the fire. I glance around for Noah and Tavvy, only to see them both knocked out on the floor behind Knox.

"We have to go! They wouldn't want you to die as well!" Sin demands, trying to pull me away.

"We have to help them!" I turn back to tell him.

"No, we have to survive and then help them. Knox and Tobias will get them out. I'm protecting you, come on," Sin demands, tugging on my arm. "Please, Madi."

"Fine," I eventually say, letting Sin drag me away through the kitchens. We run to the back of the building, hearing the explosions and screams behind us, which makes me just want to go back. I have to trust Sin though, he wouldn't leave his brothers unless there was another choice. Knox and Tobias can fight and handle themselves much better than I could anyway. I'd likely be in the way. Sin stops us in front of a door and lifts his hand, creating a sphere of fire and throwing it at the handle which melts away, and the door swings open as I kick my heels off. I can run faster without them anyway. Taking my hand again, we head out the door and start running straight across the grass to the forest ahead.

I suddenly hear the squawking of ravens and slow down, my feet sinking into the freezing cold grass as I look up at the dozens of ravens in the sky. They swirl around as Sin shouts at me, grabbing my arm, but I shove his hand away. Something is so wrong and so familiar about this all. I pull my gaze from the sky and the crows to the edge of the forest as someone steps out. Snow gently starts to fall all around us as I look into the familiar face I've longed to see for a long time.

"Quin?"

Chapter 31

"Qu-Quinton?" I manage to whisper, feeling like the entire world is frozen in this moment as he steps closer. Quin looks different, strange almost from what I'm used to. Snow falls onto his large shoulders, which have silver clips holding on a black cloak. His skin is so pale that it almost has a blue quality to it. Quinton's black hair is shorter than the last time I saw him, making him appear so much older. He looks colder yet still feels like my Quin. I instantly go to step forward, but Sin grabs my arm, and I look up at him to see him shake his head at me.

"That isn't Quin. Not anymore," Sin quietly warns me, and I flash him a confused look as the crunching of Quinton's boots on the frozen grass catches both our attention.

"Didn't you miss me, brother?" Quin sarcastically asks, taking one more step closer. The ground beneath his feet freezes each time, and it doesn't take me long to figure it out.

"You have powers," I gasp in shock. How did this happen? He is here, just like in my dreams, but it is so real. My dreams were telling me the truth, and the ravens are still circling, still loudly squawking. They are warnings, but that is all. They can't help us.

"He is a dark tale, don't you feel the need to kill him?" Sin hisses, trying to pull me away, but I stop him. This is Quin, my Quin.

"No," I whisper, my breaths coming out in clouds of cold smoke.

"You should run, Oisin," Quin warns, crossing his arms, "before this ends badly."

"Quin, this is crazy. It's us, your friends," I try to plead with him, only for him to ignore me like I'm not here. He is fixated on Sin, not really looking at me much. I don't get this. Quin has never been like this. He was kind, sweet, and I loved him.

"Things have changed," Quin tells me, his voice detached and cold, just like his powers which seem to have stopped his emotions or something. I want my Quin back, not this monster. I step closer, pushing Sin away when he tries to stop me. Quin won't hurt me, I know it. His powers and being a dark tale don't make him who he is. It doesn't make him forget our past.

"I still love you. I never stopped," I tell him, walking another step closer until we aren't far apart at all. Quin moves his eyes to me, and for a second, just a tiny second, I see my Quin in his blue eyes. I smile, going to move closer when Sin screams. The world feels paused as I turn around and see Sin on his knees. He looks down at his chest, where there is a spear of ice sticking out of the place where his heart is.

"NO!" I cry out, running across the snow and falling to my knees next to where Sin has collapsed, blood dripping into the white snow. The blood doesn't look right against the perfect white, it isn't right. I place my hands on his face, begging this all to be a dream and for him to open his eyes. He doesn't. "Sin, wake up, please. You can't be dead! You can't be! Sin! Wake up! Sin! Oisin!" I scream and scream his name until arms wrap around my body, pulling me away, but I don't stop begging for Sin to wake up. He can't be dead. He just can't be.

"Knock her out, Quinton, and send the Tale son's body to his parents. Leave a note, telling them to surrender, or I will send more of their sons' bodies." I don't look up at the man that spoke as I cry and scream Sin's name, and I struggle to escape Quin's tight grip.

"I'm sorry," Quin whispers in my ear, but I will never forgive him for this. Never. I'm almost glad when something slams into my head and darkness takes me. In darkness, there is no pain...

Epilogue

Quinton

I walk at his side through the blood-covered floors, and my eyes stay fixed on each step of his which freezes the ground, the blood turning to ice. My uncle stops at the foot of the stairwell before looking down at me. He is cruel and as cold as his powers. Powers we both have. All I can think of is Sin's expression as he died, how he looked at Madi. How Madi will never forgive me for not stopping my uncle from killing him. I push those thoughts away to focus on my only family, my uncle. I know when my uncle looks at me, he sees his dead brother—my father—and not me. So far that is all that has kept me alive. I'm not Quinton

Lupas who grew up with a girl he fell in love with and four guys who became more like brothers than best friends. I'm now Quinton Frostan, heir to the dark tales throne.

"You did well, nephew. Now we begin."

YOU CAN PRE-ORDER TALES&DREAMS (LOST TIME ACADEMY:BOOK TWO) HERE ON AMAZON... **LINK.**

Thank you so much for reading Tales & Time! I've always been a massive fan of any fairytales, and I loved bringing this world alive.

A big thank you to my family, Helayna, Mad's, Cora and everyone that supported me with this book!

A special thank you goes to Mad's for her ongoing support.

Thank you to my wonderful Pack Leaders for everything. <3

Once again, thank you readers for your continued support! You're all amazing, and I couldn't do this without you guys.

If you have a moment, please leave a review. <3

Stalker Manual

Instagram
Facebook
Twitter
Pinterest

www.gbaileyauthor.com

About the Author

G. Bailey is a USA Today bestselling author of books that are filled with everything from dragons to pirates. Plus, fantasy worlds and breath-taking adventures. Oh, and some swoon-worthy men that no girl could forget. G. Bailey is from the very rainy U.K. where she lives with her husband, two children and three cheeky dogs. And, of course, the characters in her head that never really leave her, even as she writes them down for the world to read!

Please feel free say hello on here or head over to Facebook to join G. Bailey's group, Bailey's Pack! (Where you can find exclusive teasers, random giveaways and sneak peeks of new books on the way!)

A Name Like Karma

ALSO BY G. BAILEY...

My name is Karma...and yes, it's my job too.

Since I was eighteen, I have used my powers to deliver
karma to those in need like all of my other family do.

Only they are much better at it.

I deliver much needed karma to both good and bad
humans, but mainly the bad as it's more fun.

The only rule of the job?

Don't talk to the other gods, especially not the powerful ones, and definitely don't accidentally kill one of them... *whoops.*

Now the twin gods of justice are after me, and not even my family can save me now.

If I'm caught, it will be a one ticket pass to the gods re-correction prison. It's a place where more than mere gods are locked up and no one ever escapes.

Even gods can't escape their fate...but they sure can try to run.

RH romance 17+

LINK TO AMAZON.

FIND THE FIRST CHAPTER ON MY WEBSITE-
WWW.GBAILEYAUTHOR.COM

Winter's Guardian Description

Her Guardians Series

When Winter started university with her best friend Alex, she didn't expect to find herself in the middle of a supernatural war. Who knew saving a stray wolf could earn you the alliance of the pack. To make things more complicated, the broody and very attractive Jaxson is tasked with keeping her safe from the growing vampire threat in town. It's a shame he can't stand her and enjoys irritating the hell out of her. When she finds out her new boyfriend has his own secrets, can she trust anyone anymore?

What happens when you get yourself stuck in the middle of a war?

Reverse Harem

Bonus Read

The blue-sided human will choose a side.
When four princes are born on the same day, they will rule
true.
Her saviour will die when the choice is made.
If she chooses wrong, she will fall.
If she chooses right, then she will rule.
Only her mates can stop her from the destruction of all.
If the fates allow, no one need fall.
For only the true kings hold her fate, and they will be her
mates.

"The prophecy has come true. I found out that the vampires', angels', and witches' royal sons were born yesterday," my sister says to me, a look of worry on her faultless face as I hold my little baby closer to me.

I look down at the sweet, little boy in my arms. The new shifter prince, my son and the last royal male wolf. His green eyes are glowing as he looks up at me like he holds the entire earth in his sweet eyes. I know the goddess will protect him.

"Then it's true. The goddess planned this all," I whisper.

"We must make sure they are close. Despite our wars and disagreements, the children should grow up together," she tells me, and I know she is right.

"We have a lot of planning to do, sister." I stare down at my little boy as I speak to her, "You are right, if they are to have any chance of winning the human's heart, they must be united."

"Yes, my queen." My sister bows her head at me and leaves the room. If only I could protect my child from the responsibility he now has on his tiny shoulders.

The responsibility of saving the whole world.

32

Bonus Read

"So, class, please start by reading page thirty-two in your books," the professor goes on, as my class starts after he walks in. The professor looks as ancient as the old room we are all sat in, with his brown hair and beard and very dated clothes that look like he hasn't washed them in a while. I push my own out-of-control, wavy brown hair over my shoulder, wishing I had tied it up this morning. It's a hot day, and the room is stuffy because of the lack of opened windows, making my hair stick to the back of my neck. I glance over at my best friend, Alex, who has her head on her desk, lightly snoring. I chuckle before kicking her leg and waking her up. She moves her waist-length, straight, red hair off her face to glare at me. "I was resting, Win," she mutters, hiding her eyes with her arm and huffing at me.

"The professor is here," I giggle, trying to whisper to her as she nearly falls off the side of the desk, while half asleep.

"Oh, what page?" She yawns, looking like she is going to drop back off to sleep already. I sigh, remembering how she actually has a boyfriend to keep her up all night. I, on the other hand, can't find a good one. The last time I had a boyfriend was over a year ago, and I found out he had a bad habit of sleeping around at parties. The unfortunate way I found this out was when I walked into his bedroom at his party, to find him in bed with two other girls. Let's just say he has put me off men for life, or at least for a while.

"Thirty-two," I roll my eyes at her grin.

"I might nap instead, I had a long night," she winks.

"Don't rub it in," I groan.

"Well, you're coming to Drake's party this weekend, and no, you don't have a choice. I bought you a dress, and I found you a date," she grins. I don't know which one is worse about that sentence: the fact she has bought me a dress, which I know will be way too slutty for my style, or the unlucky guy she has found for me. I decide to go with the second problem first.

"A date? You know I don't date," I hiss, while she continues to grin.

"Hey, you can't judge every man because of one. This guy is nice, a friend of Drake's." She makes that annoying face she knows I haven't ever been able to say no to since we were eight. I will never forget when I first met Alex. My mum had taken me to get an ice cream from the local ice cream van. Alex had just gotten hers in front of me, and I decided to get the same because her ice cream looked good. When the truck left, Alex tripped and dropped hers. My mum and I rushed over as she cried her eyes out over her ice cream. I offered to share mine and then, when I saw her at school the next day, we were inseparable.

"Fine, but if this doesn't go well, I'm blaming you," I laugh.

"Winter Masters, is there something wrong?" my professor asks, causing the whole class to look at me. I can hear Alex's quiet snort as I answer.

"No, sir. We were just discussing the work," I say with red cheeks. The professor raises his bushy eyebrows at me. I know he doesn't believe me. Damn, I wouldn't believe me, either. *I'm a terrible liar.*

"Well, discuss it more quietly next time, I'm sure the whole class doesn't want to know about your dating life," he replies. I hold in the urge to hide under the table at his blunt reply. A guy about my age puts his hand up at the front, drawing the whole room's attention to him. The boy has messy, brown hair that's covered up with a backwards cap. He is quite muscular under his top and shorts from what I can see. I've heard a few comments about how attractive he is, which he definitely is, but I can't remember his name.

"I would like to know, sir," he says loudly before winking at me over his shoulder. I know I'm redder than a tomato now, and one glance at Alex shows how funny she thinks this is. I'm leaving her to sleep through the class next time.

"That's enough, Harris. All of you, get back to work. I am running tests on this next week." He picks up a large pile of papers, most likely the tests he made us do last week and hasn't bothered to mark yet. I watch as he goes to his desk and pulls out his phone. I'm sure he is playing some game by the way he is typing, but he definitely isn't marking the tests.

"Also, while I remember, you need to find work experience in the next week or you'll be helping me sort out the university lost and found...for four weeks." I swear the old professor even smirked, but I didn't see him do it. I bet they would be getting him more coffees than they would be doing anything else.

"Have you heard back from the local vets yet?" Alex asks, opening her book as everyone else starts reading quietly.

"Yes, they called yesterday, and I'm all sorted." I grin, remembering jumping up and down in happiness after the call. I had applied months ago, and no one from our course was accepted, but I held out hope as I hadn't been rejected. My back-up was to work at a local farm with half our class. Studying to become a vet is hard work, and there isn't much work experience available. This is an English class, and we have to pass it to stay at the university. That's why Alex, who is a music student, is taking this class with me.

"That's great," she smiles widely, making a few guys next to us turn to look at her. Alex is that very pretty girl you always wanted to be. She is tall with boobs and hips that are perfect no matter what she eats. I look at a McDonald's meal, and my ass gets bigger. I've been told I'm pretty, but I like my food too much. So I have curves, unlike my skinny-ass best friend. My best qualities are my shiny, brown hair and blue eyes, which I have to admit, suit my golden complexion. We don't say anymore and get on with our work. At the end of class, I hand in my permission forms for the work experience, before finding Alex with her boyfriend, Drake, outside class.

"Hey, do you still need a lift?" I ask when I get close to them.

"Nope, thanks, honey. I'm going to Drake's, but I will see you tomorrow to get ready for the party." She winks, leaning against Drake. Drake is a good-looking guy but is kind of strange-looking, and I can't put my finger on why. Honestly, he looks like a typical, scary-ass man all the time. He has dark, nearly black eyes and black hair that's cut in a buzz cut, but he makes it work. It's the eyes that give him the strangeness; they are too dark, darker than I have ever seen anyone's. I always thought that he must spend a lot of time in a gym or something because he is all muscles. Alex has told me he is well off, but I knew that anyway from the car he drives and the designer clothes he wears. It's not just the looks and money, it's more how much older he acts, when he must be around twenty, like us. Alex doesn't answer many questions about him, but they have dated a while, so I'm guessing she really likes him.

"My friend is looking forward to your

date," Drake says coldly in a slight Russian accent. Alex says he's not actually from there, but his parents were, apparently.

"Me too," I lie and frown at Alex's chuckle.

"I love you, Win, never change," she says to me, as she gives me a hug before we wave goodbye. Drake doesn't say anything else, but that's normal.

I click my old, red Rover open before sliding in. My mum bought it for me as a going away present, and I love the old car, though maybe not the unusual stain on the driver seat I can't seem to get rid of; I think it's red pen. *Well, I'm hoping it is anyway.* As I drive home, I try to think about ways to get out of this date, but eventually come to the conclusion that it couldn't go that badly. *Right?*

33

Bonus Read

"You're joking, right? I can't wear this." I gesture to the tight, red dress I'm wearing. My hair is up in a messy bun with a few wavy strands around my face. My makeup is perfectly done, thanks to Alex, but I have to admit I don't look anything like myself.

"You look hot, Win," she says, pretending to cool herself down by waving her hand at her face. I look back to the mirror and glance down at the dress. It stops around mid-thigh, and the top part has a slit down the middle at the front, stopping just before my underwear, and making it impossible to wear a bra. Not that I'm worried, I'm not big chested enough to really have an issue.

"He is going to think I'm easy if I'm wearing

this," I say, sighing and turning around with my arms around my waist.

"No, he is going to think he is a lucky fucker," she laughs before straightening her own dress. Alex is wearing her little, black dress, which is a little too little but looks nice.

"Alright. But again, I'm blaming you if anything goes wrong." I laugh to myself, knowing this could only go wrong. I shut the door to my bedroom before leaving our apartment. Alex and I have a two-bedroom apartment near the university, which we rent together. It's cheap enough, and the area isn't too bad, but we still make sure we lock up.

"So, what's my date's name?" I ask as we wait outside for Drake to turn up. We are lucky the weather has been so good recently. Welsh weather is known for its constant rain, and our town is right in the middle of the mountains. Calroh is a small town but has a great university, and that's why we chose it, also the cheap apartments to rent helped. It's right in the middle of two large mountains and surrounded by a large forest. There's only one road out of town, but the town is well-stocked enough to look after itself with many large superstores.

"Wyatt. I haven't met him, but Drake speaks highly of him," she grins at me.

I think of his name for a second, trying to imagine the guy. "So, is it getting serious between you and Drake?" I ask gently, knowing Alex doesn't like to speak about relationships. Not her own at least.

"I don't know. He is so secretive that I–" she stops talking as Drake's car pulls in front us. I glance at her, and I am wondering what the end of that sentence was, but she shakes her head, smiling before opening her door. I do the same, sliding into the back.

"Hey, Drake," I say as I get in, and Alex pulls back from kissing Drake hello.

"I thought Wyatt was coming with us?" Alex asks, noticing the empty seat by me. I smile widely, hoping he is ill or isn't coming.

"He is meeting us there," Drake says bluntly before driving off.

There goes my dream of taking off this dress and changing into my PJ's, with a bottle of wine. I don't say anything, growing a little more nervous the nearer we get to Drake's apartment.

As we pull into the expensive apartment building, we can see the party has started. The music is loud, and there are cars everywhere. I mentally tell myself that going to a party at twenty years old is normal, and I should smile before getting out of the car. I walk next to Alex as Drake puts his arm around her shoulders. Just as we walk in and the loud music fills my ears, I see a blond man leaning against the wall next to the door of Drake's apartment. I can't help but stare a little at his muscular frame and his strong-looking face that I have to admit is a little scary. He seems to notice me staring and looks right at me. I first notice his eyes are that nearly black in colour or maybe just a dark-brown like Drake's. I look around, quickly noticing that nearly every girl nearby is watching the breathtaking guy like I am. My eyes draw back to his, noticing how powerful he looks. He can't be more than twenty-five but looks like he owns the very street he is standing on. The guy's eyes never leave mine as I look him over, and I shiver from the anger I feel in his eyes. *How can someone look so serious and cold at our age?* I continue walking with Alex until we stop in front of the guy, and I want to get to know him or hear him speak. My mind and body feel drawn to him, and I don't like it.

"Drake, this must be my date," the man says in a dark, underwear-dropping voice, nodding at Drake before looking back at me. I feel myself blush as his gaze takes in all of me slowly. I do the same, noticing for the first time that he is wearing a black jumper with black jeans, which look like they were custom-made for him; they possibly were.

"Wyatt. It's nice to meet you, Winter," he offers his hand. I take his cold hand, and he shocks me by bringing it up to his mouth and placing a kiss on the back. His lips feel cold on my hand, but I feel a strange shock when his lips meet my skin. It takes everything in me not to pull my hand away and run in the other direction like my body is screaming for me to do. For some reason, I don't feel safe with him.

"Nice to meet you, too," I mutter a slight lie, pulling back my hand.

Wyatt just flashes me a knowing look before saying to Drake, "There was a problem tonight, they are getting braver," his deep voice gets stronger about whatever they are discussing. It's almost like his voice draws you in and demands that you listen.

"Just a few newbies chasing a pup, it's being dealt with," Drake smiles with a cold look in my direction.

"Good. Now, can I get you a drink?" Wyatt asks looking back at me. It's strange to see how Wyatt spoke to Drake then. It was like a boss ordering around an employee, and worse, I had no idea what they were speaking about. *What's a pup?* Maybe it's a kind of business talk, I doubt they mean a puppy.

"Sure," I say taking his open arm and letting him guide me through the house. I can feel how cold he is, even through his jacket. I look back to see Alex, who has disappeared with Drake. Knowing Alex, I bet they already left, thinking Wyatt seems nice, while I don't feel that he is at all. He seems too haunted to be described as nice. Seeing how he just spoke to Drake makes me more distrusting of him.

"Are you cold?" I ask, noticing that it's a hot summer day in May. I'm even warm in a little dress, and he is cold in a jumper.

"Just cold-blooded," he winks at me. I can't help but blush a little, but who wouldn't when a very hot guy flirts with you. I know I need to act normal for a bit, before making an excuse and leaving. We weave through the hallways of the building and up two floors in the elevator which is filled with couples making out. I watch as they stop and stare at Wyatt like he is a god and ignore me completely. It's all very odd.

"So, tell me, what do you study?" he asks as we enter the kitchen. It's a modern kitchen with many cabinets that don't look used, and there's even a bar on the one side next to an impressive window. There are a few people around, but it's quiet enough in here to not have to talk too loudly. Wherever the loud music is coming from, it's not nearby.

"I'm studying to become a vet. What about you?" I look over the view of the nearby forest and mountains as he hands me an opened beer. I don't like beer, but I'm not telling him that, so I pretend to drink it.

"The family business," he says, still looking at me. He moves closer, so I have to lift my head up to look at him.

Being so short can be really annoying at times, I think to myself. This guy has at least a foot on me, and I feel small around him. Now that he is closer, I can see that his eyes are definitely black with little silver sparks in them. I've never seen eyes like his, and they are really stunning. I clear my throat before asking, "Have you known Drake long?"

"Yes, it feels like I've known Drake forever, sometimes," he grins at me like I'm missing a joke.

"I feel like that with Alex, sometimes," I say, looking away because his eyes are so stunning that they draw you in. The other door in the room opens as a drunken man stumbles in; he quickly leaves again when he sees Wyatt but leaves the door open. Now I can see the living room, well it's more a dance room. The dancing bodies are pushed so closely together that you can't see their faces. The music is beating hard and fast compared to the slow-moving young people swaying around. I turn back to see Wyatt watching me closely.

"Dance with me? You seem like you need to

relax," he asks. I lift my head to stare into his eyes, and I feel the need to dance with him, to do anything he wants. I stare at his eyes as he smirks, moving closer to me. I could have sworn his eyes had silver sparks, nothing like the empty, black pits I'm staring into now.

I shake my head, stepping back. "No thanks, I don't dance," I say to Wyatt's cold gaze. This time, his face converts into confusion, and he steps closer to me than before. We are almost touching with how close he is.

"Dance with me, Winter," he says looking into my eyes again, his eyes glowing far brighter than they should. I yelp when he grabs my arm roughly. I take a step away. His grip is strong, but I realise he isn't trying to hurt me. I don't dare look away from him as the black, glowing eyes stare into me, like he is looking into my soul.

"No, let go, Wyatt," I say firmly, challenging his grip by struggling away. I don't know what changes, but he lets me go with an utterly confused and shocked look marking his handsome face.

"How is that possible?" he mutters to himself, running his hands through his hair, and stepping away from me. I take the chance he gives me to run out the door, not caring who is looking. I have a feeling challenging a scary man like that is not a good idea. I don't think running from him is a good idea either, but, hey, it's all I have right now. *I couldn't have seen glowing eyes, right?* I mean, that doesn't even make sense to me, it must have been a trick of the light or something. I eventually make my way outside. I can't believe my luck when I spot the guy from class, Harris, opening his car door for a young girl to get in. I'm glad I remembered his name now.

"Wait, Harris!" I shout from the door, and he turns to me, looking a little shocked, but more worried than anything else.

"Are you alright?" he asks, none too gently as he grabs my shoulders, pulling me closer, and looking me up and down.

"Yes, but I could use a lift home," I say gently as I pull away from him a little, enough that he drops his warm hands.

"Sure, I was just taking my sister home. My parents are going to kill her for sneaking out tonight. So, I'm sure she needs some extra time to come up with a decent excuse," he laughs, opening the back door for me.

As I get in, I look behind me to see Wyatt watching me from the door. I swear I'll never forget the look he has on his face as he watches me get into the car. He is looking at me like he is a starving man, and I am his meal. I gasp before slamming the door shut and closing my eyes for a second, resting my head against the cold leather.

"So, what's your name?" the girl in the front asks the minute I get in. I smile as I hear her draw out the question. I open my eyes to see a pair of light-blue ones sparkling at me.

"I'm Winter, and you are?" I put on my seat belt as Harris gets in.

"I'm Katy. How do you know my brother?" she smiles, but it looks cheeky.

"You should be thinking of excuses to help yourself, and not asking questions," Harris answers her question as he looks at me in the rear-view mirror. I smirk at him when I see he is trying not to laugh, and he winks at me.

"They are going to ground me for life anyway," she says to Harris with a huff and looks back at me. "So, do you have a boyfriend?" she asks, clearly not concerned about her parents, and I look her over now. She has the same light-brown hair as Harris and matching blue eyes, that are lighter than most. I would guess she is around sixteen, making her way too young to be here. She is wearing a purple dress that is as short as mine but makes her look a hell of a lot older than she is. I can see why Harris's parents are going to be mad. I'm guessing the amount of makeup she has on isn't going to help her case. She doesn't need it, though; I can see under it all that she is very pretty.

"No. I'm escaping a bad date, actually," I mutter as she laughs.

"Harris should ask you out, he wouldn't be a bad date," she winks, and I see Harris blush.

"I'm not dating anymore, but if I were, Harris would be a good choice," I say gently, letting them both down easily.

"You should change your mind. You're really pretty." She sighs, finally turning around. Harris asks for the address, so I give it to him before opening my phone. I'm surprised not to see any messages from Alex, and I send her a quick one:

Date was awful, shame the hot ones are always crazy. I got a lift home. I will see you tomorrow. Love you xx

I missed out on the start of the argument as I was texting, but from Harris's angry face, he isn't happy.

"There are loads of them around right now, Katy. I don't want to find you sneaking out again," he shouts, leaving me to wonder what he is talking about. Katy is looking tense in her seat at whatever it is.

"I know. But I never get to leave the pack," she

says, looking out the window with a long sigh. I'm sure that I see tears in her eyes as she picks her nails, looking worried.

"It won't always be like this, but please, for me, don't leave again without one of us." He stares at her for a moment, and I see her lower her gaze quickly.

"I promise," Katy says with a frown, and Harris nods, looking back at the empty road. I watch as he turns to look at me, and a grin lights up his face when he sees what I'm wearing. Typical guy, but at least he has the common sense to look back at the road after a second, not voicing his opinion.

"What's a pack?" I ask, clearing my throat and hopefully my red cheeks from Harris's stare. I remember reading about packs of wolves in class, but I don't think they are talking about that. Maybe it's some kind of gang or a name of a house; I don't want to guess because I'm sure I'm going to come up with something worse than what it actually is. I glance at Harris who isn't answering my question, so I repeat myself.

"Oh, it's nothing important," Harris says quickly, all the while he is glaring at Katy like a parent whose kid just told someone a big secret of theirs. I glance back at Katy, who looks very guilty, as she shrugs at me, and avoids looking at Harris at all. This night is proving to be all kinds of confusing, and I'm pretty sure forgetting it is the easier way. No one says anything else while we drive home, and a tense silence descends on the car.

"Are you going to be okay to walk in? I don't think I can get in the car park with the gate down." Harris looks at me, as he stops on the road outside my building. The whole building is close to the university, so it has to be on lock down after a certain time, and you can only walk in, past a locked gate. I'm lucky the gate's broken, so you don't need a key to get in. Well, unlucky in certain ways because it means anyone can get in.

"Yeah, I'll walk in. The gate is open," I say to Harris, and he nods, watching me closely like he wants to say something, but I get out of the car before he can.

"Bye, Katy, and good luck with your parents," I say through the open window, and I laugh, hearing her grumble before I move away from the car. I wave them both off before opening the broken gate to the locked car park, the door is slightly open anyway from our neighbours.

The car park is almost as big as the building in length, and you have to walk across the whole thing to get to my building. My building has three flats, on three levels, and we have the bottom one. The car park is empty besides my car and one other. I walk slowly; only the dim lights of the street lamps near the building are lighting my path, showing me where I'm going. In the distance, I notice a big, dark shape lying next to my car, near the door to my building. I run over quickly, my footsteps being the only noise in the dark night. I'm hoping the person is okay and pull my phone out of my bag as I run, ready to call an ambulance, but as I get closer, I see it's a wolf.

Could my night get any weirder?

34

Bonus Read

I slowly move forward to get a closer look, slipping my phone back in my bag. I'm a little relieved to see it's not a big wolf. The wolf is the size of a small child and has light-brown fur, or it could be black, but I can't tell in the dim light. The light catches against the large dagger stuck in its back leg. I hear him whine as he looks up at me with dark eyes, I don't feel like he could attack me if he tried, so I carefully move closer. I know how dangerous it is, and Alex would kill me for this, but there's a reason I wanted to be a vet. I love helping animals, I've been helping injured animals since I was a little girl, and I brought home a cat that had been run over. So, there's no way I can leave this wolf now, no matter how foolish it might seem.

"Hey you, look, I'm a vet," I say in a calm,

soothing voice, and then think to myself that I should leave out the in-training part.

"I can help you, but you can't hurt me, or I will have to leave you alone, alright?" I say gently, hoping my calming tone of my voice soothes him enough that he will trust me. The wolf must be smart because I swear he is listening to every word and hasn't growled at me once yet. He might be someone's pet, as he doesn't seem to be scared of me like most wild animals are of humans. I don't know why I'm suddenly calling this wolf he, it might be a girl for all I know.

The wolf whines at me, so I take that as a yes. I know I can't take him to a vet or they might put him down. Even if he is tame, most vets won't help him. The wolf is a wild animal that is usually hunted in other countries, but I can't just do nothing. My mum would be going mad right now; like the time I brought home another injured cat that was a local stray, and it chased me around the house when it woke up, trying to bite me. That cat was not thankful for my help.

I crouch down on my knees, carefully turning my phone light on to look more closely. The wolf is nearly all black, as I run a hand over his fur and pull it back because he is mostly covered in blood. I know I need to pull this dagger out and then get him inside to stitch it up. I'm lucky I have some stuff in my emergency medical box that I can use.

"Alright, handsome wolf, I'm going to pull this out and then get you inside to my apartment. I can stitch this up for you," I say to him. I swear that he actually blinks at me as an answer.

"Please don't hurt me for this," I mutter and quickly pull it out with a shaky hand, and he yelps loudly. I'm surprised when he doesn't growl at me, and I could swear little tears are coming out of his eyes as he collapses to the ground.

"Shush, I'm so sorry, little wolf," I say gently as I stroke his neck. He passes out after a few seconds, which is likely from all the blood loss. I'm hoping he is strong enough to make it through this, because I have no idea how much blood he could have lost just getting here. I stand up, looking down at the wolf, and think through my options quickly. I know, with him unconscious, I can get him back to my flat without making too much noise or distressing the poor creature.

I look at the knife in my hand; it's heavy, and I think it's real silver as it shines in the moonlight, the blood dripping off it looking unnatural and scary. It has unusual drawings all over it that I don't recognise, but they look very much like crowns. I put it in my handbag with my phone, shutting off the light.

I'm lucky I'm kind of strong because carrying the large wolf the short walk to my ground floor apartment is almost killing me. I eventually get to my door, opening it before carrying the wolf into my lounge and placing him on the floor. I lean against the wall, getting my breath back, and look down at my red dress now covered in blood and stuck to me with sweat. I put the lights on and walk out to grab the first aid box out in the kitchen. When I come back in, I scream.

I must be going crazy because where I left the wolf, there is now a young boy around eight or so, curled up in a ball, with a mop of black hair with blond tips covering his face, and he's naked. I rush over to him, seeing how pale he is and looking around for the wolf in my small lounge. The front door is shut, so I know he didn't get out, but as soon as I'm close to the boy, his body shakes before he shifts back into the black wolf.

I scream again, dropping the box on the floor, and just stare at the passed-out little wolf.

What the hell? I know I'm having a really bad night, but I really didn't think I had gone completely mad. I slide to the floor, staring at the wolf, and I remember some weird things. Like all the books I read as a teenager about werewolves, and now there is a real one in my living room. Who knew they were actually real? *Should I be running out of the room, screaming?* The image of the small boy appears in my mind as I look at the wolf, and I realise that I don't care what he is, he needs my help.

I eventually calm myself down. Knowing that the wolf is only a child and needs help, no matter what he is, helps me do that. I go closer to see the stab wound, and I'm surprised it is looking better, as it's nearly all sealed up. I decide to grab a blanket from my room and cover the wolf up to the neck, just in case he turns again. I'm guessing the fast healing must be a wolf thing. I do eventually think of the downside of having a supernatural creature in my house—what if others that are like him come looking for the child and think I hurt him? I should run, but I don't, because I can't leave a child without knowing for certain he is okay.

I've always been the type to do a massive cleaning when I'm stressed. Alex is the kind that cooks everything, like my mum does, but Alex doesn't make anything edible or without a high risk of food poisoning. I get some bleach and water, then start scrubbing the floor up to the door where there is blood and outside my door too, before locking it.

I check on the wolf, and I'm not that surprised

to see it's the boy again, but it still looks like he is sleeping. I go to my room, taking off the now blood-covered dress and putting on some casual clothes. I avoid looking at myself in the mirror because that would make this night way too real for me, and I want some answers from the boy before I do that.

I get a wash cloth out of my bathroom, getting it a little wet before going to the boy.

"Hey, I'm just going to clean you up a little," I say to him. Even if he isn't awake, I'm hoping he can hear me. I can still hear his yelp when I pulled that dagger out, who would hurt a little child like that?

I clean his face and then his shoulders. I lift the blanket to look at the dagger wound on his lower leg. It's nearly all healed, so I clean it up carefully and put a bandage on it before covering his leg up again.

I sit down on the couch, looking at the boy, wondering what the hell to do now. It's not like I can call a doctor to explain I have a boy that changes into a wolf sometimes. Or would I call a vet? I eventually lie down on my couch and drift off to sleep.

KARMA

My name is Karma…and yes, it's my job too.

Since I was eighteen, I have used my powers to deliver karma to those in need like all of my other family does.

Only they are much better at it.

I deliver much needed karma to both good and bad humans, but mainly the bad as it's more fun.

The only rule of the job?

Don't talk to the other gods, especially not the powerful ones, and definitely don't accidentally kill one of them… Whoops.

Now the twin gods of justice are after me, and not even my family can save me now.

If I'm caught, it will be a one-way ticket pass to the gods' correctional prison. It's a place where more than mere gods are locked up and no one ever escapes.

Even gods can't escape their fate...but they sure can try to run.

17+ RH

Bonus Read

I speed around the corner of the empty road just in time to see a swarm of bees fly straight into John on the bike. The helmet does little to hide his pure panic as the swarm attacks him. He screams and lets go of the handles of the bike to no doubt pull the helmet off where the bees must have gotten inside. The bike rapidly turns, heading straight into a barrier of the cliff. Like it's a damn movie, everything slows as John is flung off the bike as it crashes into the barrier, and he goes flying into the air over the very large and steep cliff. I slam on the brakes on my bike in a panic, letting it fall to the ground as I set off running to the barrier, expecting to see a flat and very dead John at the bottom of the cliff. I breathe out a sigh of relief when instead I see John holding onto a branch, hanging over a very dirty looking pond at the bottom of the cliff. It's one hell of a drop, though. Poor John is having a very bad day.

"HELP!" he screams at me. "Please help me!"

"Yep, I'm coming!" I shout back at him, climbing onto the barrier and getting to the other side. I pull my charms out, finding the one for rope. It's a plain flat circle, but if you look closely, you can see the never ending rope that is tied inside it. I shake the circle sphere a few times, pretending that John's screams aren't getting louder and more desperate. I glance down at him, seeing his beefy arms that make his head look ridiculously small in comparison. It's okay, he can hold himself up for sure. The sphere spreads out into a bigger flat circle after a few shakes. I reach into the silver shimmering liquid inside the circle to pull out a long piece of magic rope that will never end. John continues to scream, like that is helping anybody, as I tie the rope to the barrier and the other part around my waist.

"For the love of gods, can you be quiet? I need a moment of silence to talk myself into this as I don't like heights," I shout to John, who doesn't seem to care one bit as he continues to scream. I shake my head, wondering why I'm bothering when I could leave the douchebag to fall into the pond. It looks deep enough for him survive the fall. *Possibly.* No, I'm the better person, and I can't just walk away from this when I'm pretty sure this is all my fault. Or at least that is how my family will see it when they find out. I turn myself around while muttering about how high the drop is before forcing myself to start walking down the rocks, lowering myself on the rope as I go. I don't know how long it is before I get near John, and he straightaway grabs my ankle. The grip is so strong that I cry out from his weight.

"Wait a second, don't do that!" I shout at him, trying to shake him off as he pulls on my leg, trying to climb up me. *I'm no rope, dude.* The idiot lets go of the branch altogether, wrapping both his arms around my legs, and the rope drops us a tad. I scream, trying to shake him off as the rope slips from my hands, cutting into them as I desperately try to hold his weight up with mine. This is not what I had planned. What kind of feckin' gobshite is he? He is going to kill us both.

"Do I look like a bodybuilder who can hold your weight as well as my own, you feckin' eegit!" I shout at John, who is screaming and shaking as he holds onto my legs, completely ignoring me. My first hand slips just before I can do nothing but shriek as the rope falls from my hands, somehow letting me fall through the rope tied around my stomach. As I fall through the cold air, I brace myself to hit the pond water just as someone slams into me. I open my eyes, seeing my brother floating in the air above me, struggling to hold us all up with a shiny barricade of blue light. He holds a spear in his hand, and the tip glows the same blue as the barrier. My brother and his magical stick to the rescue again.

"Karma Maria Kismet. Give me your friggin' hand."

Ah crap.

35

Bonus Read

I lift the heavy jug of water in the air, letting it pour all over the face of my best friend as she snores in bed. I chuckle as she coughs, letting out a tiny scream and rolling off the side of her single bed, pulling the red sheets off with her.

"Karma, have you lost your god damn mind?!" she shouts, huffing and puffing as she sits up, wiping her face.

"You told me to do it! Remember?" I say, reminding her of what she asked me yesterday. " 'If I don't wake up for the job interview, you have full permission to pour ice cold water over my face to get my lazy ass up,' " I mimic her voice as she still glares at me.

"Did you even try to wake me up the normal

way?" she asks as she stands up, picking up her bedsheets as she does.

"Nope, but I have coffee," I say, knowing that will distract her into forgiving me. I'm pretty sure my bestie, Mads, has been addicted to coffee since I've known her. We met in school when we were both eight years old. Mads grins, running past me to the cup of coffee in the travel mug on her counter. She sighs as she takes a long sip and then goes to grab a towel.

"Why is this job interview so feckin' important?" I ask her, sitting on her messy bed as she towel dries her hair.

"Unlike *some* people, we don't all live rent free in our parents' house and have no job, Karma," she sarcastically states, though I know she doesn't mean it in a nasty way. I do have a job, not one that she could ever find out about though. I couldn't even imagine telling Mads I'm a goddess of karma and get paid in pure gold to deliver karma to the world. I also don't think she would believe me if I said I hide my box of gold at the end of a rainbow, as rainbows are the safest bank storage in the magical world. Don't even get me started on how protective our family leprechaun is. My mum went all literal by naming me what my family's job is. My brothers all have normal names, but oh no, mum and dad had to choose Karma for me. I'm named after my great ancestor, the original karma goddess.

"I will get a job, you know, when I run out of money," I say, which will be never because being a karma god is a job I will have to do until I die. The higher gods make sure we are well paid though, better than any human job could pay us, to make sure we would never leave our work. I know there have been gods and goddesses who have left—or tried to—only to find themselves thrown into the gods' correctional facility. I shudder. That place is worse than any nightmare a god of dreams could give you.

"You are so lucky," she says with a longing sigh, disappearing into her wardrobe to get dressed. Mads doesn't have family, and her foster parents let her runaway to Dublin at fifteen, and they never looked for her. She kept in contact with me though, only as I wouldn't let her just disappear on me. Decent friends are hard to come by and even better if they don't ask too many questions like her. Mads has worked a million jobs to keep her tiny studio flat and food on her table, and I admire her for it. I really hope she gets the job today; I know there isn't much food in her fridge, and she won't let me help her out with money. I push my curly, waist-length red hair behind my ear as I stand up and go to the mirror as I wait for her. I glance down at my black leather leggings and black vest top that shows a little bit of my stomach off.

"You still look like a sexy Irish Barbie doll, don't worry," Mads jokes, and I turn to grin at her, seeing her smart work uniform that suits her curves, long blonde hair which she has pulled up into a bun. We are both Irish, though somehow Mads has a stronger accent than I do, and her curse word list is pretty impressively mixed between British and Irish words.

"Coming from the actual Barbie doll with big boobs," I reply, because she damn well looks like one of those little feckers she used to steal from me as a kid. "Though you look great, and you will be fine today."

"What are your plans for today?" she asks, and I glance down at my hand, seeing the name John Markson in black ink tattooed on the back. I flip my hand over, seeing the black Celtic circle knot in my palm, which when touched will take me to wherever John Markson is so I can deliver his karma. When the ink is black, it's my favourite kind of karma to deliver. The bad kind. Usually I ignore the ones that are gold, because I'm not the type to give good things to people all the time. My brothers and parents are much better at those jobs.

"I have a date with a John Markson," I say as honestly as I can. It won't be a date, more of a bad surprise depending on what I can sense he hates the most. It will be funny either way.

"Sounds like fun," she says, winking at me before grabbing her bag and leaving her apartment. I turn my hand over and press the mark, disappearing into a puff of green dust.

36

Bonus Read

*W*hen I reappear, shaking the green dust off my clothes, I look around at the street that I'm in. Each house is a good distance apart and filled with massive mansions protected by big metal gates stopping anyone from getting in. I'm taking a wild guess the house right in front of me is my guy, judging by the fact it is the biggest on the row. Usually, rich guys need a good dose of bad karma because they are born dickheads. That isn't always the case, but years of this job have taught me those born with a silver spoon in their mouths tend to think they can do what they want with no consequences.

I walk across the street, pull the mailbox in the brick wall open, and look for a name on the letters inside. *John Markson.* Perfect. I shove the letters back in before going to the gate and pulling my necklace out of my top. I flip past the lucky charms until I find the magic key charm and press the key against the metal gate. It glows purple for a second before the gate swings open. *This is going to be easy.* I love my lucky charm necklace; there is not much that my charms can't do. Each charm was a birthday gift from my parents over the years. The important ones are on my necklace, and the less important ones are on an ankle bracelet of mine. All twenty of them have been useful somehow over the years, or they have got me into trouble somehow. Either way, my necklace keeps things fun.

I walk up the expansive driveway, admiring the flower beds that my mum would adore. I pass some very nice cars that I have no idea what they are, but man, would one of my brothers love them. I jog up the rest of the driveway, which is straight uphill, and I'm out of breath by the time I get to the top of it. *Maybe I should go to some of those cardio classes with Mads.* I straighten up once I get my breath back and look at the posh manor house. There is loud music coming from inside, and two motorbikes are parked outside the house in pride position. Clearly this guy loves his bikes, maybe his fear is they get stolen or something. I could make them disappear for sure.

I walk up to the front door and turn the handle

to find that it is open. That's some good luck right there. I try not to whistle as I sneak into the white tiled entrance hall and see the white walls with a surfboard hanging on the wall by the stairs. The place is posh, like the kind of house a celebrity would live in. Everything from the vase of vivid flowers in the middle of the entrance hall to the art deco painting of a beach on the one wall makes me think this guy has a lot of money.

I follow the noise of the music and pause outside a closed door, knowing I don't need to make him aware I'm here. Sometimes it is better to get a feel for the karma I need to deliver rather than actually working out if the person is a good guy or not. I close my eyes, calling on my karma powers to sense if the guy I want is in there and what exactly he is scared of. It doesn't take more than a second to feel him close, close enough for his deepest fear to slip into my mind. I get an image of bees, dozens of bees attacking a child that I bet was him when he was younger. Well, this should be funny. Bees are highly intelligent insects, and I like them. They won't attack you unless you piss them off first or attack their home. Luckily, there is another way to get them to attack someone. I flip through my charms, finding the animal calling one which looks like a fox, and grin. A swarm of bees is pretty bad karma if you are scared of them. I lift the charm to my lips and press a kiss onto the silver metal.

"I call a swarm of bees to help me in my time of need. A man is due a karma kiss. Come to me, it is my only wish," I finish off my call, and the charm glows a bright green before rapidly fading. Thank god I'm good at rhyming, considering half the charms will only work with a rhyme for some odd reason. I'm pretty sure it's because my parents got the charms second hand at a magic stall at the magical market. Though we have money that would be considered a good amount for humans, it is pennies to the rest of the magical world. We are on what they call minimum wage that simple gods and goddesses like us get paid to make the world keep going, but it is a hell of a lot of money. I cross my arms, leaning against the side of the door as I listen to his god awful choice in music. It's now time to wait for my handiwork to play out. Usually the bees don't take too long to get here, and my family will be hella impressed that I did a job without messing it up as usual.

I freeze as the door opens in front of me, and a man walks out, holding a pair of keys in his hand. Crap, this is my guy, and there is no way I can let him get in a car right now, but I also can't explain why I'm in his house. I wait until he walks out the door before running after him, pushing the door open and jogging outside to see him get on the back of a motorbike. Double shite. That little eegit is going to get himself killed...and I will get the bloody blame.

"Stop!" I shout, but the sound of his engine's revving hides my shout, and he speeds off down the road. I glance over at the spare bike resting on the side and know I don't have a choice at this point. I need to catch up with him and make sure he is on the ground when those bees come. I can't let another guy get way without bad karma because he is too injured, and then have to call my family for help. A swarm of bees attacking him while he is on a bike is only going to cause a big problem for me.

I run to the bike, swinging my leg over it, and turn the key. Thank god for that bad boy dating stage I had at eighteen. Darren, the dickface, as I decided to name him, may have slept with my science teacher, but at least he taught me how to ride his bike before I found out. I quickly speed down the driveway, just sliding through the closing doors before they shut on me. That might have hurt otherwise. The wind whips against my ears, no doubt making my hair more wavy and messy. I swing the bike to the left, turning down the street where I can see John disappearing into the distance.

I speed up, trying to chase him as he heads onto another road and disappears around a corner.

I speed around the corner of the empty road just in time to see a swarm of bees fly straight into John on the bike. The helmet does little to hide his pure panic as the swarm attacks him. He screams and lets go of the handles of the bike to no doubt pull the helmet off where the bees must have gotten inside. The bike rapidly turns, heading straight into a barrier of the cliff. Like it's a damn movie, everything slows as John is flung off the bike as it crashes into the barrier, and he goes flying into the air over the very large and steep cliff. I slam on the brakes on my bike in a panic, letting it fall to the ground as I set off running to the barrier, expecting to see a flat and very dead John at the bottom of the cliff. I breathe out a sigh of relief when instead I see John holding onto a branch, hanging over a very dirty looking pond at the bottom of the cliff. It's one hell of a drop, though. Poor John is having a very bad day.

"HELP!" he screams at me. "Please help me!"

"Yep, I'm coming!" I shout back at him, climbing onto the barrier and getting to the other side. I pull my charms out, finding the one for rope. It's a plain flat circle, but if you look closely, you can see the never ending rope that is tied inside it. I shake the circle sphere a few times, pretending that John's screams aren't getting louder and more desperate. I glance down at him, seeing his beefy arms that make his head look ridiculously small in comparison. It's okay, he can hold himself up for sure. The sphere spreads out into a bigger flat circle after a few shakes. I reach into the silver shimmering liquid inside the circle to pull out a long piece of magic rope that will never end. John continues to scream, like that is helping anybody, as I tie the rope to the barrier and the other part around my waist.

"For the love of gods, can you be quiet? I need a moment of silence to talk myself into this as I don't like heights," I shout to John, who doesn't seem to care one bit as he continues to scream. I shake my head, wondering why I'm bothering when I could leave the douchebag to fall into the pond. It looks deep enough for him survive the fall. *Possibly.* No, I'm the better person, and I can't just walk away from this when I'm pretty sure this is all my fault. Or at least that is how my family will see it when they find out. I turn myself around while muttering about how high the drop is before forcing myself to start walking down the rocks, lowering myself on the rope as I go. I don't know how long it is before I get near John, and he straightaway grabs my ankle. The grip is so strong that I cry out from his weight.

"Wait a second, don't do that!" I shout at him, trying to shake him off as he pulls on my leg, trying to climb up me. *I'm no rope, dude.* The idiot lets go of the branch altogether, wrapping both his arms around my legs, and the rope drops us a tad. I scream, trying to shake him off as the rope slips from my hands, cutting into them as I desperately try to hold his weight up with mine. This is not what I had planned. What kind of feckin' gobshite is he? He is going to kill us both.

"Do I look like a bodybuilder who can hold your weight as well as my own, you feckin' eegit!" I shout at John, who is screaming and shaking as he holds onto my legs, completely ignoring me. My first hand slips just before I can do nothing but shriek as the rope falls from my hands, somehow letting me fall through the rope tied around my stomach. As I fall through the cold air, I brace myself to hit the pond water just as someone slams into me. I open my eyes, seeing my brother floating in the air above me, struggling to hold us all up with a shiny barrier of blue light. He holds a spear in his hand, and the tip glows the same blue as the barrier. My brother and his magical stick to the rescue again.

"Karma Maria Kismet. Give me your friggin' hand." Ah crap. I smile up at Peyton as he shouts his demand, sounding just like mum when she is mad as hell. I reach up, slamming my hand into his just as John, the moron, pulls hard on my leg as he screams. My leg slams through the magical barricade, my hand slipping from Peyton's, and there is nothing to stop us as we all fall into the dirty water. I swim up to the surface, gasping air into my lungs as I wipe my eyes to see John come up right in front of me. He screams as he sees me, like I'm not the person that just tried to save his sorry ass. How ungrateful. A second later, my brother's head appears out of the water to my right, and he looks like he just wants to murder me. Fair enough, I can't actually blame him.

"Hey, bro...how are you?" I awkwardly ask. "I see you had a haircut…"

"Why am I always saving your arse, Karma?" he asks, glaring at me before swimming towards the edge of the pond. After a while, I see that Peyton pulls himself out of the pond and shakes his long red hair of the green water before crossing his arms. I shrug before turning around and swimming to the end of the pond, a bit away from him as I'm not stupid, and pulling myself out. My clothes are ruined, and I hold in a squeal as I pull out a small fish from my hair and throw it back in the pond.

"I didn't need any help. The pond broke our fall," I point out as I see Pey looking at me like I should be saying sorry or thank you. I don't know which one he expects, but he isn't getting either.

"Y-you were flying!" John shouts, saving me from having to say anything at all. John screams at Peyton as he gets out of the water and then starts running into the forest in front of us. I look at Peyton, and we both burst into laughter, neither one us able to stop laughing for a little bit.

"See, it's not all bad. Just a little mess up, and I could have handled it," I say when the laughter dies off.

"That pond has sharp rocks at the bottom, and it would have killed you if you fell without me stopping you," he points out. "Now I'm going to find whoever that screaming idiot is, wipe his memory, and then we can get going. I feckin' stink, Karma."

"I didn't know he was going to fall off a cliff, now did I?" I say, squeezing the pond water out my hair as Peyton walks past me.

"Somehow, you never seem to have any blame for every job that goes wrong," he tells me. "Lucky you have a family to get your arse out of trouble, isn't it, little sis?"

"I don't mess up every job," I point out. "It's like one out of five, and I think that's pretty good."

"Not for a karma god, sis," he reminds me. "Now your guy is going to forget today, including his bad karma and get away with whatever he did. Without true karma, the world would be ruined. You need to get better at this." With his gloomy warning that makes me feel bad, he jogs into the forest after poor John. I lie back on the grass, looking up at the rocky cliff and bright blue sky. At least it's a nice day for John to have gone swimming.

**Four Dragon Guards. Three Curses. Two
Heirs. One Choice...
Forbidden love or the throne of the
dragons?**

Isola Dragice thought she knew what her future
would bring. Only, one earth-shattering moment
destroys everything.

When war threatens her home, Isola returns from
earth to the world of dragons she knows nothing
about, and to Dragca Academy.
When the four most powerful dragon guards in
history are ordered to protect her, they didn't expect
to be protecting an accident prone princess. One
who, accidentally, nearly kills her whole class at
Dragca Academy in her first week.

What happens when fire falls for Ice?

18+ **Reverse harem romance**

Book One of Five.

Bonus Read

Everything inside me screams as I run through the doors of the castle, seeing the dead dragons lining the floors, the view making me sick to my stomach. I try not to look at the spears in their stomachs, the dragonglass that is rare in this world. *Where did they get it?* The more and more bodies I pass, both dragon and guards, the less hope I have that my father is okay. *No, I can't be too late, I can't lose him, too.* The once grand doors to the throne room are smashed into pieces of stone, in a pile on the floor, and only the hinges to the door still hang on the walls. I run straight over, climbing over the rocks and broken stone. The sight in front of me makes me stop, not believing what I'm seeing, but I know it's true.

"Father . . .?" I plead quietly, knowing he won't

reply to me. My father is sitting on his throne, a sword through his stomach, and an open-mouthed expression on his face. His blood drips down onto the gold floors of the throne room, and snow falls from the broken ceiling onto his face. There's no ice in here, no sign he even tried to fight before he was killed. He must not have seen it coming; he trusted whoever killed him.

"No," is all I can think to say as I fall to my knees, bending my head and looking down at the ground instead of at the body of my father. *I couldn't stop this, even after he warned me and risked everything.* I hear footsteps in front of me as I watch my tears drip onto the ground, but I don't look up. I know who it is. I know from the way they smell, my dragon whispers to me their name, but I can't even think it.

"Why?" I ask, even as everything clicks into place. I should have known; I should have never trusted him.

"Because the curse has to end. Because he was no good for Dragca. Our city needs a true heir, me. I'm the heir of fire and ice, the one the prophecy speaks of, and it's finally time I took what is mine," he says, and every word seems to cut straight through my heart. *I trusted him.*

"The curse hasn't ended, I'm still here," I

whisper to the dragon in front of me, but I know he can hear my words as if I had just spoken them into his ear.

"Not for long, not even for a moment longer, actually. Your dragon guard will only thank me when you are gone. I didn't want to do this to you, not in the end, but you are too powerful. You are of no use to me anymore, not unless you're gone," he says. I look down at the ground as his words run around my head, and I don't know what to do. I feel lost, powerless, and broken in every way possible. There's a piece of the door in front of me that catches my attention, a part with the royal crest on it. The dragon in a circle, a proud, strong dragon. My father's words come back to me, and I know they are all I need to say.

"There's a reason ice dragons hold the throne and have for centuries. There is a reason the royal name Dragice is feared," I say and stand up slowly, wiping my tears away.

"We don't give up, and we bow to no one. I'm Isola Dragice, and you will pay for what you have done," I tell him as I finally meet his now cruel eyes, before calling my dragon and feeling her take over.

37

Bonus Read

"Isola!" I hear shouted from the stairs, but I keep my headphones on as I stare at my laptop, and pretend I didn't hear her shout my name for the tenth time. The music blasts around my head as I try to focus on the history paper that is due tomorrow.

"Isola, will you take those things out and listen to me?" Jules shouts at me again, and I pop one of my headphones out as I look up at her. She stands at the end of my bed, her hands on her hips, and her glasses perched on the end of her nose. Her long grey hair is up in a tight bun, and she has an old-style dress that looks like flowers threw up on it. Jules is my house sitter, or babysitter as I like to call her. I don't think I need a babysitter at seventeen,

318 • TALES & TIME

not when I'm eighteen in a while anyway, and can look after myself.

"Both headphones out, I want them both out while you listen to me," she says. I knew this was coming. I pull the headphones out and pause the music on my phone.

"I did try to clean up after the party, I swear," I say, and she raises her eyebrows.

"How many teenagers did you have in here? Ten? A hundred?" she says, and I shrug my shoulders as I sit up on the bed and cross my legs.

"I don't know, it's all a little fuzzy," I reply honestly. My head is still pounding; it was probably the wine, or maybe the tequila shots. *Who knows?* I look up again as she shakes her head at me, speaking a sentence in Spanish that she knows I can't understand, but I doubt it's nice. I don't think I want to hear what she has to say about the party I threw last night anyway. I look around my simple room, seeing the dressing table, the wardrobe, and the bed I'm sitting on. There isn't much in here that is personal, no photos or anything that means anything to me.

"Miss Jules, looking as beautiful as always," Jace says, in an overly sweet tone as he walks into my bedroom. He walks straight over to Jules and kisses her cheek, making her giggle. Jace is that typical hot guy, with his white-blonde hair and crystal-blue eyes. Even my sixty-year-old house sitter can't be mad at him for long, he can charm just about anyone.

"Don't start with that pouty cute face," she tuts at him, and he widens his arms, pretending to be shocked.

"What face? I always look like this," he says, and she laughs, any anger she had disappearing.

"I'm going to clean up this state of a house, and you should leave, you're going to be late for school. I don't want to have to tell your father that as well, when I tell him about the party," she says, pointing a finger at me, and I have to hold in the urge to laugh. She emails my father all the time about everything I do, but he never responds. He just pays her to keep the house running and to make sure I don't get into too much trouble. If he hasn't had the time to talk to me in the last ten years, I doubt he's going to have the time to email a human he hired. Jules walks out of the room, and Jace leans against the wall, tucking his hands into his pockets. I run my eyes over his tight jeans, his white shirt that has ridden up a little to show his toned stomach, and finally to his handsome face that is smirking at me. *He knows exactly what he does to me.*

"You look too sexy when you do that," I comment, and he grins.

"Isn't that the point? Now come and give your boyfriend a kiss," he teases, and I fake a sigh before getting up and walking over to him. I lean up, brushing my lips against his cold ones, and he smiles, kissing me back just as gently.

"We should go, but I was wondering if you wanted to go to the mountains this weekend and try some flying?" he asks. I blank my expression before walking away from him and towards the mirror hanging on the wall near the door. I smooth my wavy, shoulder-length blonde hair down, and it just bounces back up, ignoring me. My blue eyes stare back at me, bright and crystal-clear. Jace says it's like looking into a mirror when he looks into my eyes, they are so clear. I check out my jeans and tank top, and grab my leather coat from where it hangs on the back of the door before answering Jace.

"I've got a lot of homework to do–" I say, and he shakes his head as he cuts me off.

"Issy, when was the last time you let her out? It's been, what, months?" he asks, and I turn away, walking out through my bedroom door and hearing him sigh behind me.

"Issy, we can't avoid this forever. Not when we have to go back in two weeks," he reminds me, and I stop, leaning my head back against the plain white walls of the corridor.

"I know we have to go back. We have to train to rule a race we know nothing about, just because of who our parents are. Don't you ever want to run away, hide in the human world we have been left in all these years?" I ask, feeling a grumble of anger from my dragon inside my mind. I quickly slam down the barrier between me and my dragon in my head, stopping her from contacting me, no matter how much it hurts me to do so. *I can't let her control me.*

"Issy, we were left here so we would be safe. We are the last ice dragons, and our parents had no choice. Plus . . . being a dragon around humans is a nightmare, you know that," he says, stepping closer to me.

"I don't want to rule; I don't want anything to do with Dragca," I say, looking away.

"I guess it's lucky we have each other, ruling on our own would have been a disaster," he says, stepping in front of me so I can't move and gently kissing my forehead.

"I know. I just don't want to go back to see my

father and everything that has to come with it," I say, and he steps back to tilt my head up to look at him.

"You're the heir to the throne of the dragons. You're the princess of Dragca. Your life was never meant to be lived here, with the humans," he says, and I move away from him, not replying because I know he sees it differently than I do. He is the ice prince, and his parents call him every week until they disappeared when he was twelve and he knows they loved him. I haven't spoken to any of my family in ten years, and I have never stepped back into Dragca since then. It's the only thing we disagree on, our future.

"Issy, let's just have a good day, and then, maybe, I could get you that peanut bacon sandwich you love from the deli?" he suggests, running to catch up with me on the stairs.

"Now you're talking," I grin at him as he hooks an arm around my waist, and leans down to whisper in my ear.

"And maybe later, I could do that thing with my tongue that you—" he gets cut off when Jules opens the door in front of us, clearing her throat, and ushering us out as we laugh.

"*L*ittle Issy, are you coming to my party this weekend? I know I'd love to show you my house and–" Michael asks as he stops me outside my English class, but I'm not listening to whatever he is saying. When I hear the bell ring, relief that it's the last class of the day fills me. Learning human things all day isn't fun, especially when you know you won't ever need to know any of it. The only class I love is my study period, where I can go to the library and find a new book to live in. I lift my bag on my shoulder and look around Michael for Jace, not seeing him anywhere. I look down at my arm as Michael steps closer, and he strokes a hand down it, making me shiver, but not in the good way.

"I don't know, I would have to ask Jace and see if he wants to go, but I don't think he likes you. Also, I'm not little, short is a better word," I say plainly, wanting to get as far away from Michael as possible. Michael is a good-looking human with black hair and is covered in tattoos, which I usually find attractive, but my dragon still wants to eat him, so even being friends with him would be a disaster. Plus, Jace would kill him if he saw how Michael was touching my arm. Dragons see their future mates as treasures, precious, and they don't share often.

"He doesn't own you; you could come alone," Michael snaps, clearly not happy I don't want to sneak off to his stupid frat-boy party.

"Why would I do that?" I ask the idiot football player, as I try to move away. I shove his hand off my arm, turning and walking away before he can reply.

"Because you're so much better than him. Come to my party!" he shouts at me, and everyone stops to look at us. They begin whispering, stupid rumours that will spread around the school by tomorrow. I don't even know Michael really, he's just another human I grew up with, and I know he isn't acting like himself. It's the dragon side of me that is attracting him, and every male human in this damn school. That's why I have always stayed close to Jace's side; male dragons have the opposite effect on humans. All the humans are scared of him here, everyone except for Jules. I stand on my tiptoes as I look around, before remembering Jace's last class was sports management on the other side of the building. I walk out of the school, going around the main entrance and see the gym across the field. I walk slowly across it, just thinking he must have had a shower or something after class, and he is running late. I stop dead in my tracks when I pick up an unfamiliar scent in the mixture of human smells. I smell a dragon, a fire dragon that shouldn't be here.

"Let me out," my dragon hisses in my mind. I slam the barrier down again, holding my head when she fights me, making me have to stop running towards the gym.

"Enough, Jace needs me!" I shout at her in my head, and she stops fighting instantly as she realises that I won't let her out and I can't help Jace like this. Overwhelming worry for Jace is the only thing coming from her as I run, and it floods my own emotions, nearly strangling me with panic. I run towards the door, push it open, and run across the small room that leads to the gym. I open the doors and immediately freeze at the sight in front of me, until a loud scream rips from my throat, and I fall to my knees. Even then, I can't believe it, not until the pain threatens to strangle me, not until I can't see anything other than the truth that is lying right in front of me.

"NO!" I scream out, my dragon's roar following my words as her sorrow and shock mixes with mine. In the middle of the room is Jace, a large red dagger sticking out of his heart, his head is fallen to the side, facing me with wide eyes in the dimly-lit room. I can't look away from his eyes, open in shock as blood drips from his mouth and makes a tiny noise as it hits the floor. I force myself to look away from his eyes, only to look at the blood that makes a circle around him, so much blood that pours from the wound. I crawl across the gym floor, tears running from my eyes, and I don't stop, even as my hands get covered in his blood once I get to him. I pull his head onto my lap, stroking a blood-stained finger across his cheek.

"No! Jace, baby, wake up. Please don't do this to me," I plead, my hand shaking against his cheek as he remains still. I know he is dead, my dragon and I both know it, but I can't believe it. Everything in me feels like it's breaking into a million pieces. I hear footsteps behind me, but I can't look away from Jace, as I raise my hand and close his eyes, leaving bloody fingerprints on his eyelids. I take a deep breath, committing to memory the smell of the fire dragon that did this to Jace.

"I vow revenge, I vow to never let this be forgotten. I will always love you," I whisper, my tears falling onto his face as I press my forehead to his, and then scream and scream, until my throat cracks.

"Don't. Let her say goodbye, we have time," I hear a male voice say behind me. I turn and look over my shoulder, the shock from everything just seeming to merge together as I see my father standing at the door. Ten royal guards stand around him, and his ice-blue eyes watch me. There's no sorrow or remorse in my father's eyes, not that I honestly expected anything else from him.

"Time to leave, there is nothing to be done here, Isola," he tells me. I look back at Jace, not wanting to let him go, but knowing my father's suggestion to leave wasn't really a suggestion at all. I have to go; whoever did this to Jace would kill me in a heartbeat.

"Isola, we must leave. Danger is near," my father warns me once more, and I gently rest Jace's body on the floor.

"I love you, and I'm so sorry I wasn't here. That I couldn't save you," I whisper. As I lean down and kiss Jace's cold cheek, another sob escapes me, and I wipe my eyes.

"Give him a true dragon's burial, or I will not leave," I warn my father as I stand up, blood sticking to both my clothes and my hands. I step back, seeing a young guard my age come to stand next to me. I look up into his hazel eyes, the only part of his body that I can see, thanks to the black uniform that covers his head and all of his body.

The only other colour is the ice-blue dragon crest over his heart. All the dragon guards wear uniforms like this in the human world, and what I remember of them in Dragca is not much different.

"You have my vow," he says, and something makes me believe him as we stare at each other. I step back, turning and walking over to my father after one last look at Jace. My father stands tall as he holds a hand out for me, like I'm a child that needs his comfort. I ignore his hand and stand in front of him, feeling the dragon guards close ranks around us.

"I am sorry we were late, we didn't know of the threat until it was too late," he says. I don't say a word, I can't. Jace is dead; my dragon mate and the dragon I was meant to marry. We should have run away, not stayed here.

"What will be done now? There are no ice dragons other than you and me," I comment, needing to focus on anything other than the broken feeling in my heart, as the smell of smoke fills the air. The dragon guard will be burning Jace's body, and the thought makes me want to crumble onto the ground.

"Remember that our bodies are just shells for our dragons, that Jacian will be free to fly the night skies, and you will see him again one day," my father offers advice, and I still stand completely silent. I watch tiny red sparks float into the air around the gym, the soul of Jace leaving this world. They disappear slowly; each time they go, it shatters me a little bit. *No words will take away the pain that is crushing my heart.*

38

Bonus Read

"*T*ell me, what happened today? How did Jacian end up dead?" my father asks me in a disappointed tone, as we walk through the forest behind my home and towards the portal to Dragca. I look down at my red coat, wondering which student the guard stole it from as I pull it closer around myself. I look down at my still blood-covered hands, Jace's blood, and I almost trip on a rock as the image of his dead body flashes into my head. *He is really gone.*

"Why don't you tell me why you are here early? Did you know this would happen?" I ask him, knowing it's no coincidence that he turned up early, just as Jace was killed. *My Jace is gone.* As I wipe more tears away, I think about how I won't be able to kiss him again, how I won't be waking up next to him anymore. The boy I grew up with, fell in love with . . . is gone.

"I asked first," he replies, and I turn to look over at him as he walks at my side. My father's white hair is cut short, his white crown sparkles in the sun. He has a black cloak that slides across the ground, with blue embroidered edges and the dragon crest on the chest. He looks every bit the king I remember, but not my father.

"Nothing abnormal happened, it was a normal day," I reply, looking forward again, I feel the portal magic as we draw closer.

"What of Jules?" I ask, after he doesn't reply to me for a long time.

"Who?" he answers with a question, and I shake my head with a low laugh. I was right, he never read a single one of the hundreds of emails, or checked in on me once over the years. I used to pretend that he couldn't come to me because it wasn't safe, and that maybe he was watching me from a distance. Or talking to Jules about me. *I guess I was wrong.*

"The house sitter, the woman you left me with, the one who brought me up?" I ask, trying not to snap at him.

"Oh, we have left a decent amount of human money for her, she is now retired, which I'm sure she is happy about," he waves me off, clearly not caring at all.

"I wish I could have said goodbye," I say quietly.

"She is just a human, they would not care for goodbyes if they knew what you really are, Isola. Plus, we have bigger issues to focus on," he says, stopping the conversation, and I smile tightly. I'm guessing feelings are not something my father cares about.

"Fine. How did you know we were going to be attacked?" I ask him.

"The royal seer had a vision, a dragon death, but I didn't know which one of you or what time it would be. We came as soon as possible," he replies, his tone is so calm, as he talks about his only child possibly dying, or the man she was due to mate with. I look away as tears start slowly falling down my cold cheeks, wiping them on my coat.

"You must not cry anymore, you must be strong as we return to Dragca. Enemies watch us at all times," he scolds me as I continue to cry. A feeling of numbness spreads over me, just holding myself together until I can be alone and let my feelings out. He has a point, I know my life is in danger, and I can't die now. Jace will have died for nothing if I die, too, and no one would remember him like I do.

"You can't tell me how to feel," I snap, feeling my dragon weeping in my mind. She doesn't even try to contact me anymore, just sits quietly, and that is very unlike her. She feels like I do, broken, and I don't put the barrier up between us, letting her emotions mix with my own.

"I am not telling you what to feel, only how to act. You are Isola Dragice. The powerful princess we have waited for," he grabs my arm to stop me walking. "Act like it. Don't shame Jace's memory," he tells me firmly, and all the guards stop to wait for us as we stare at each other. I look into my father's frosty blue eyes, the coldness of them having nothing to do with the ice dragon inside of him. He is just cold-hearted, just like I remember him being. I never had the loving father, and I don't expect that from him now. It still stings that he demands what I do, how I should act, when he knows nothing of me.

"Are we going to the castle?" I ask, changing the subject, and shoving his hand off my arm. He pauses, looking down at me strangely for a second, before turning away.

"No, we are going to Dragca Academy. The castle is not safe enough for you at the moment. The academy is, and you must learn about your world before you take the throne," he says, making me go silent. It was never the plan to go to Dragca Academy; a school full of fire dragons is no place for an ice dragon like me.

"Father, I was meant to take the throne in two weeks, what has changed?" I ask.

"I will explain more when we get to Dragca," he replies, looking around at the dragon guards. I nod in understanding. He doesn't want to tell me when so many of the dragon guard could hear. I pause as I spot the portal, a yellow wall that shimmers in between some tall trees that look like all the others here. Humans cannot see it, and even if they got close, the portal naturally pushes them away. It makes them want to get away from it at all costs, even scaring the weak-minded humans. Some humans with strong minds have made it through the portal, but they can never find a way to return, and life in Dragca as a human isn't easy.

"In formation, the king and princess follow two guards through, and the others behind," a guard next to my father shouts, and we get into a line at his command. The guard in front whispers to the portal, telling it where we need to go. The guards keep their swords at their sides as we each walk towards the barrier. My father steps through in front of me, and I stop, freezing as a memory of when I last went through a portal flitters into my mind.

"*You* *ou have to let go now," my father says, as I clutch his hand tightly and force myself to let go. He walks through the portal, and I follow, trying not to jump at the cold feeling. I pull my cloak closer around myself as I walk towards my father where he is speaking with two guards.*

"Take her to the house, and then travel a fair distance away before coming back to Dragca," he tells the guards. I look up at the snow falling from the sky, it lands on my nose, and I wipe it away as I wait.

"Go with them, Isola," my father tells me, not even looking my way, as he walks around me and towards the portal.

"Wait! Father, what is going on? Where are you going?"

"I have a world to rule, and you must stay here, stay alive. We will see each other again, Isola, and I will send information with the ice prince," he says, and I run after him only to be caught by a guard and picked up.

"Father, don't leave me like mother, please don't!" I scream, wiggling and trying to get the guard to put me down. My father looks back at me one more time, no compassion or anything loving for me to remember, as he disappears. I realize

that not only did I lose my mother that year, but also my father.

"Your highness?" a guard says, pressing a hand on my shoulder, and I quickly shake myself out of the memory that haunted me for years, the heartless father who left me here in the human world and acted like I was forgotten. Jace was sent to me a few months later, with boxes of books and information on dragons. He got me to leave my room for the first time in a long time. He made me laugh, and explained that my father only did what he did to keep me safe. I step through the portal, feeling the cold magic push against my body, and then I open my eyes to the home I've not seen since I was eight.

Dragca Academy is right in the middle of the snowy mountains, and the only way to get in is to use a portal or fly. The academy, itself, is a huge castle with three towers, three levels of balconies for dragons to land on. There is a stone path leading to the doors, a side building with a stone battle field outside, which is covered in weapons in metal hold-ers. There is what looks like an arena behind the castle, but I can't tell from here. I spot three other dragons walking around and one flying over the mountains in the distance, but they are only shadows from here. I look up at the stars, knowing it must be late here. Time is opposite on Earth and Dragca, as are the seasons and just about everything you can think of. Dragca has two suns and two moons in the sky. I look around to see the two moons, the large one and the tiny one by its side.

"My King," a woman says, distracting me from staring, and I turn around to see her walking down the steps of the castle. She has a dark-blue cloak on, the royal crest on a silver pin holding the cloak together. She lowers the hood, her long dark-red hair falling around her shoulders. She smiles widely as I try to think why she looks so familiar to me.

"Esmeralda, it is a pleasure to see you. You're as beautiful as I remember," my father says, taking her hand and kissing it, and I mentally roll my eyes when she laughs sweetly at him.

"It has been many years since you married my sister, and yet you are still the charmer," she says, making me remember why she looks so familiar now. She is my step-aunt and the headmaster of Dragca Academy, if I remember right. I remember them being called the ice and fire twins, one born of ice and the other of fire. A rare birth in our world, nearly impossible, and apparently it shocked all of Dragca. I read about them in one of the books my father left, as I was interested in the step-mother I had only met two months before I was sent to Earth. All I remember about her is her long, perfect white hair, and how cruel she was to the maids and dragon guards in the castle. My father married her not long after my mother died because she was the last female ice dragon alive other than me. They soon found out she couldn't have chil-dren, making me and Jace the only heirs to the throne left. The only ice dragons left. Now there are three: my father, me, and my stepmother.

"And yet you still look as beautiful as all those years ago. My wife sends her love," he says, and she rests her hand on his arm in an overly affectionate way. I'm pretty sure my stepmother wouldn't like that her sister seems so familiar with her husband. But then, I don't really know anything about them.

"Come in, we have a lot to discuss. Where is Jacian?" she asks, her eyes finally landing on me.

"Dead," I reply, almost robotically, as I stand completely still.

Esmeralda's hand flies to her mouth, "I am so sorry, Isola."

Part of me believes her, but I can't think about it. I look away as we all start walking quietly towards the castle. I blink and do a double take when I see a man standing in the shadows under one of the towers. He's dressed in all black, and I'm sure he is a guard, but for some reason, I can't stop staring at him as he moves closer. He lifts his hand, and I catch a glint of silver before he throws it at us.

"Get down!" I scream, slamming into my father, and we fall to the ground as the dagger lands in the heart of the guard on his right. The guard falls to the ground in front of us, as the other guards form a tight circle around us and pull their swords out. The guards quickly make a circle of fire around them, the heat blasting against my skin.

"Five to the left, two on the right," my father says, sniffing the air.

"When I say the word, run to the doors and get inside," my father tells me. He grabs my chin with his hand when I don't answer, "Do you understand, Isola?" he asks, and I nod despite the shock.

"Now!" he shouts, throwing his hands in the air and shooting ice in every direction except the one I'm running in. Ice and dragonglass, are the only ways to kill a fire dragon easily. Fire cannot kill an ice dragon, that is what makes us different and stronger. Only dragonglass can—and our own ice, not that we would use our ice on ourselves. *That wouldn't be smart.* The fire wall parts when I get close, closing behind me as I run straight to the closed stone doors.

"Duck, princess!" I hear a man shout from my left, and I turn my head to see a man dressed in the all-black guard uniform running at me. He has black hair that's cut short and shaved at the sides, his lip is pierced with a ring, and the man is built like an actual god. *Or like a rock star from Earth.* I'm too busy staring at the guy to stop him when he slams into me, both of us landing on the floor as a dagger flies past us.

"What part of 'duck' do you not understand?" the man asks, rolling us over, so he is on top of me. He looks down at me, placing his hands near my head as he rolls his lip ring between his lips, somehow frowning at me at the same time.

"Get the hell off of me, who do you think you are?" I ask him, watching as he smirks at me.

"Dagan Fire, nice to meet you princess. Now stay down, or I might as well kill you, myself," he says as he jumps off me in a fluid motion, pulling a red dagger out of his belt and throwing it. I roll on to my stomach to see the dagger land in the forehead of one of the attackers, and the body slams to the floor. When I turn back over, Dagan holds a hand out for me.

"You don't have to say thank you," he says as I accept his hand to pull me up.

"I was going to," I reply, and he grins, still holding my hand as we stare at each other.

"I am one of the dragon guard, your kind doesn't say thank you to us. We die for you royals every day. We are just soldiers, and soldiers don't get thanked as they die," he says, giving me a sarcastic smirk as he drops my hand and steps away. I watch him look around, following his gaze to the five dragon guards lying dead, some from my father's ice that is everywhere, and others from dragonglass daggers.

"Now get inside, princess," Dagan demands, pissing me off, and I step closer, looking up at him.

"Dagan Fire, thank you for saving my life, but if you tell me what to do again, we will have a big problem," I tell him, and before he can reply, my father steps next to me. Dagan looks away, his jaw grinding in annoyance.

"Bring the bodies inside, I want to know who dares to attack the king and princess," he tells Dagan, who nods as he steps back and turns around. My father puts his hand on my back as he walks us inside the castle, and I don't look back once.

Made in the USA
Monee, IL
16 July 2023